2024

Zentrale Prüfung

Original-Prüfungsaufgaben
mit Lösungen

Gymnasium · Gesamtschule NRW

Englisch 10. Klasse

STARK

1. Auflage
www.stark-verlag.de

Inhaltsverzeichnis

Länderporträts zu den Bezugskulturen

Hinweise, Tipps und Übungsaufgaben zu den Prüfungsbereichen

Sobald die Original-Prüfungsaufgaben 2023 freigegeben sind, kannst du sie als PDF auf der Plattform MyStark herunterladen (Zugangscode vgl. Umschlaginnenseite, vorne im Buch).

Audio-Dateien

Listening Tests 1–4
Zentrale Prüfungen 2021–2023

Sprecher*innen: Eva Adelseck, Daniel Holzberg, Rees Jeanotte, Veronica Stivala
Auf die Audio-Dateien kannst du ebenfalls über die Plattform MyStark online zugreifen.

Sollten nach Erscheinen dieses Bandes noch wichtige Änderungen in der Prüfung vom Ministerium für Schule und Bildung in NRW bekannt gegeben werden, findest du Informationen dazu auf MyStark.

Autor*innen
Markus Hözel-Fröndgen: FAQs, Übungsaufgaben, Lösungen zu den Originalprüfungen (Wortschatz und Schreiben)
Sandra Klüser-Hanné: Länderporträt Neuseeland, Martin Paeslack: Lösungen Originalprüfungen (Hör- und Leseverstehen), Redaktion

Vorwort

Liebe Schülerin*lieber Schüler,

mit diesem Übungsbuch hast du die Möglichkeit, dich Schritt für Schritt selbstständig auf die ZP 10 in Englisch vorzubereiten und mit allen Übungsformaten und den Themenbereichen vertraut zu machen. Diese Prüfung ist wichtig, weil ihr Ergebnis 50 % deiner Zeugnisnote in Klasse 10 ausmachen wird.

Zunächst gibt dir das Buch einen Überblick über die gesamte Prüfung, v. a. was den **Aufbau** und die **Gewichtung** der Prüfungsteile betrifft, und beantwortet häufig gestellte Fragen.

Daran schließen kompakte Hintergrundinformationen in Form von **Länderporträts** zu den sogenannten **Bezugskulturen** der Prüfung 2024 an: **Großbritannien und Neuseeland**. An dieser Stelle aber die beruhigende Nachricht, dass in der Prüfung *kein* konkretes Wissen über diese beiden Länder abgefragt werden wird.

Zu allen **Kompetenzbereichen** der Prüfung (Hörverstehen, Leseverstehen, Wortschatz und Schreiben) erhältst du einen Überblick über **Aufgabenformate** und **nützliche Strategien** zur Bewältigung sowie viele **Übungsaufgaben im Stil der Prüfung** mit hilfreichen Bearbeitungshinweisen und **anschaulichen Lösungsvorschlägen**.

Am Ende des Bandes findest du **Original-Aufgaben** der zentralen Prüfung aus den Jahren **2021** und **2022**, ebenfalls mit Lösungsvorschlägen. Auf die Original-Prüfung **2023** kannst du online zugreifen.

Ich wünsche dir viel Freude beim Training in der Vorbereitung und viel Erfolg, Gelassenheit und Ruhe in der Prüfung!

Markus Hözel-Fröndgen

Markus Hözel-Fröndgen

Hinweise zu den digitalen Zusätzen

Auf alle **digitalen Inhalte** dieses Buches kannst du online über unsere Plattform **MyStark** zugreifen. Deinen persönlichen **Zugangscode** findest du auf der Umschlaginnenseite, vorne im Buch.

PDF der Original-Prüfungsaufgaben 2023

Um dir die Prüfung 2023 schnellstmöglich zur Verfügung stellen zu können, bringen wir sie in digitaler Form heraus. Sobald die Original-Prüfungsaufgaben 2023 freigegeben sind, kannst du sie als PDF auf der Plattform MyStark herunterladen.

Audio-Dateien

Die Hörtexte aller Aufgaben stehen dir als **MP3-Dateien** zur Verfügung.

Hilfreiche Wendungen – Web-App „MindCards“

Mit der Web-App „MindCards“ kannst du Wortschatz am Smartphone einüben. Auf den **interaktiven Lernkarten** findest du nützliche Formulierungen für den Prüfungsteil Schreiben sowie für mündliche Prüfungen.

Die Lernkarten sind für den Einsatz am Smartphone gedacht, können aber auch am Desktop-PC, Laptop oder Tablet verwendet werden. Scanne die QR-Codes oder nutze die Links, um die Web-App zu starten:

*https://www.stark-verlag.de/mindcards/**speaking**-1*

*https://www.stark-verlag.de/mindcards/**writing**-1*

Interaktives Training

Das Online-Training „**Basic Language Skills**“ bietet dir zahlreiche interaktive Aufgaben aus den Bereichen **Wortschatz** und **Grammatik**. Dies sind ganz wichtige „Basics“, die du für eine gute Sprachbeherrschung brauchst.

FAQs – Häufig gestellte Fragen zur ZP 10

Wie ist die Prüfung aufgebaut?

Die Prüfung in Englisch besteht aus **zwei Teilen mit mehreren Aufgaben in unterschiedlichen Kompetenzbereichen**, von denen einige in der Gewichtung besonders relevant sind.

- Im ersten Teil der Prüfung wird das **Hörverstehen** in zwei Aufgaben überprüft.
- Im zweiten Teil werden **Leseverstehen**, **Wortschatz** und **Schreiben** überprüft.

Wieviel Zeit habe ich für die Prüfungsteile und wie ist die Bewertung?

Insgesamt hast du ca. 120 Minuten Zeit für die Bearbeitung aller Prüfungsteile, wobei bei der Schreibaufgabe noch 10 Minuten „Orientierungszeit" dazukommen.

Die Punkte, die du für die Aufgaben erhältst, werden am Ende in Prozentpunkte umgerechnet. Die folgende Tabelle gibt dir Aufschluss über Zeitvorgaben und Gewichtung der Bereiche:

Prüfungsteil	Zeit	Kompetenzbereich	Prozentanteil der Gesamtnote
1	ca. 20 Min.	Hörverstehen	15 %
2	ca. 100 Min. + 10 Min.	Leseverstehen	15 %
		Wortschatz	10 %
		Schreiben	**60 %**

Was genau bedeutet „Orientierungszeit“ bei der Schreibaufgabe?

In der dritten Aufgabe im Bereich „Schreiben“ gibt es eine Auswahlmöglichkeit zwischen zwei Aufgaben. Hierfür stehen ungefähr 10 Minuten zusätzliche Entscheidungszeit („Orientierungszeit“) zur Verfügung.

Wann findet die Prüfung statt?

Die Prüfung im Schuljahr 2023/24 findet in NRW voraussichtlich am Donnerstag, **16. 5. 2024** statt. Der offizielle Nachschreibtermin ist am Dienstag, **4. 6. 2024**.

Darf ich während der Prüfung ein Wörterbuch benutzen?

Nein, die Verwendung eines ein- oder zweisprachigen Wörterbuchs ist nicht gestattet. Aber keine Sorge, selbst wenn Wörter vorkommen, die du noch nicht kennst, kannst du diese oft aus dem Zusammenhang erschließen. Außerdem ist es gar nicht notwendig jedes einzelne Wort zu verstehen, um die Aufgaben richtig zu lösen.

Gibt es inhaltliche Schwerpunkte? Was bedeutet „Bezugskulturen“?

Die inhaltlichen Themen bzw. Schwerpunkte der Aufgaben orientieren sich an den Vorgaben der Kernlehrpläne Sek I, v. a. aus dem Unterricht der Jahrgangsstufe 10. Der Fachunterricht bereitet also inhaltlich auf die Prüfung vor.

In der Prüfung gibt es zwei englischsprachige Kulturräume („Bezugskulturen“), die vorgegeben sind, und somit im Fokus stehen: derzeit **Großbritannien und Neuseeland**. Es ist aber *nicht* notwendig, landeskundliches Wissen (auswendig) zu lernen, da dieses *in keiner Weise* abgefragt werden wird. Einige Grundkenntnisse zu den Kulturen können aber helfen, sich allgemein sicherer und vorbereitet im Umgang mit den Texten der Prüfung zu fühlen. Hier helfen die Länderporträts auf den nächsten Seiten. Zusätzlich gibt es viele Übungen im Band, die sich inhaltlich konkret auf die beiden Kulturen und die Themenfelder des Kernlehrplanes beziehen. Die behandelten Themen sind immer zu Beginn einer Übungsaufgabe angegeben (bei *Listening Test 1* beispielsweise „gesellschaftliches Engagement“ und „Berufsorientierung“)

Wie unterscheidet sich die ZP 10 am Gymnasium vom MSA an Gesamt- und Realschulen?

Die Aufgaben zum **Hörverstehen** und zum **Leseverstehen** sind in der ZP 10 am Gymnasium und beim Mittleren Schulabschluss gleich. Die Aufgaben in den Bereichen **Wortschatz** und **Schreiben** sind je nach Schulart individuell.

Zusatzinfo: An den Gymnasien fand in Zeiten von G 8 keine ZP 10 mehr statt. Einige wenige Gymnasien in NRW sind damals nicht zu G 8 gewechselt und hatten deshalb wie die Gesamt- und Realschulen eine ZP 10. Ab 2024 findet wieder für alle Schüler*innen in G 9 an allen Schulformen flächendeckend eine ZP 10 in NRW statt.

Wer korrigiert meine Prüfungsarbeit?

In der Regel korrigiert als erstes deine Englischlehrkraft deine Prüfung. Anschließend korrigiert diese eine weitere Fachlehrkraft deiner Schule. Die beiden bilden dann die Note gemeinsam.

Wie genau setzt sich die Note im Abschlusszeugnis zusammen?

Die Abschlussnote Englisch deines Zeugnisses setzt sich zu 50 % aus der Jahresnote (= Vornote aus beiden Halbjahren) und zu 50 % aus der Note der ZP 10 zusammen:

- Stimmen Jahresnote und Prüfungsnote überein, ist die Jahresnote auch die Zeugnisnote. Bei einer Abweichung von einer Note entscheidet deine Englischlehrkraft mit dem*der Zweitkorrektor*in deiner Prüfung über die Zeugnisnote.
- Sofern deine Vornote und deine Prüfungsnote um zwei Noten abweichen, hast du das Recht, eine freiwillige mündliche Prüfung zu absolvieren. Deine Zeugnisnote wird dann wie folgt berechnet:

  50 % Jahresnote, **30 %** ZP 10, **20 %** mündliche Prüfung

  Der Prüfungszeitraum hierfür ist zwischen dem 18. und 27. 6. 2024
- Sollte deine Prüfungsnote um mehr als zwei Notenstufen von der Jahresnote abweichen, ist diese mündliche Prüfung verpflichtend. Deine Zeugnisnote wird dann wie folgt berechnet:

  50 % Jahresnote, **30 %** ZP 10, **20 %** mündliche Prüfung

  Der Prüfungszeitraum hierfür ist ebenfalls zwischen dem 18. und 27. 6. 2024

LÄNDERPORTRÄTS

Länderporträts zu den Bezugskulturen

Some aspects about the UK

The United Kingdom consists of the island of Great Britain (England, Scotland, Wales) and Northern Ireland. It is also informally referred to as "Britain" or "the UK". The British flag, the so-called **Union Jack**, is a combination of the English, Scottish and Northern Irish flags.

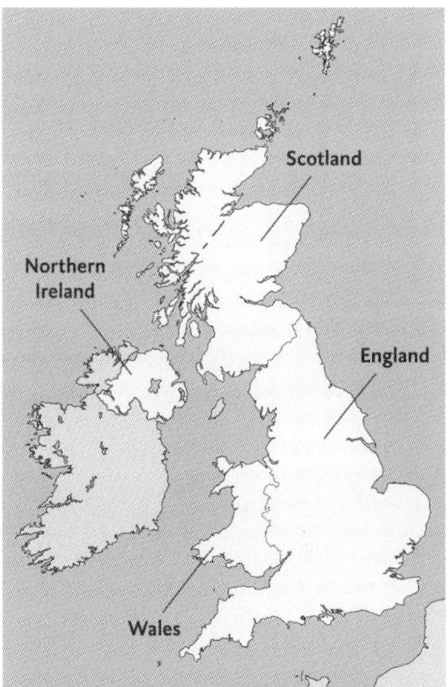

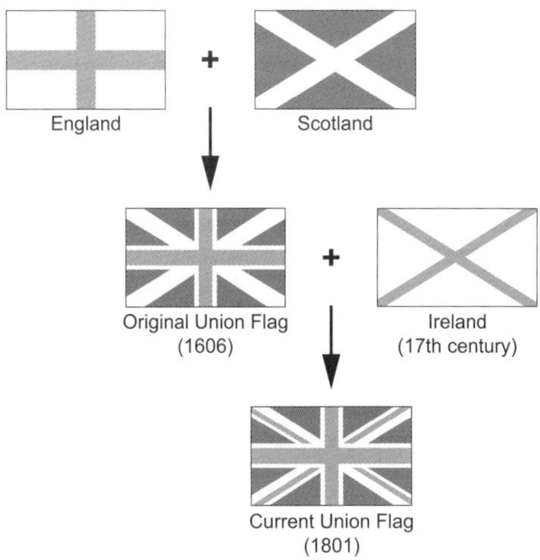

- **Political system:**
  The UK is a parliamentary democracy with a constitutional monarch. The King is the official head of state, and although he has quite a few political functions, his role is mainly ceremonial. The members of the **royal family** are important

identification figures, however, as can be seen, for example, in the heartfelt sympathy following the death of Queen Elizabeth II.
Most of the actual political power in Britain lies in the hands of the **Prime Minister and his or her cabinet**, who have a relatively dominant position and can take far-reaching decisions. The work of the government is controlled by **Parliament**, which is made up of two chambers: the House of Commons (consisting of elected Members of Parliament/MPs) and the House of Lords (consisting of bishops or "peers" who either inherited their seat or were nominated by the monarch). MPs are elected by means of a **majority vote** or "first-past-the-post": The candidate who wins a simple majority of the votes in a constituency *(Wahlkreis)* becomes the MP for that district; the votes for the other candidates are ignored. This system tends to benefit big parties (such as the Conservatives or the Labour Party) and makes it relatively hard for smaller parties to win seats. In 1998, some power was handed over from the central parliament in London to regional parliaments in Scotland, Wales and Northern Ireland, a process known as "**Devolution**".

- **From the Empire to the Commonwealth:**
  For several centuries, Britain was an important imperial power that colonised and exploited other countries. At the beginning of the 20th century, the **British Empire** covered over a quarter of the world's surface. From the late 19th and early 20th century onwards, however, more and more countries wanted to break free from British rule, and after India gained its independence in 1947, the empire gradually came to an end. After decolonisation, a lot of former colonies maintained some ties with Britain and joined the so-called **Commonwealth of Nations**, a loose and voluntary organisation of over 50 independent states. They cooperate economically and politically, share the same values (such as democracy and human rights) and are connected by the English language.
  As a result of Britain's imperial past, English is now spoken in many parts of the world – it has become a **lingua franca** that allows speakers with different native languages to communicate with each other. Other cultural "exports" from Britain include its political system, famous works of literature (e. g. by William Shakespeare or Charles Dickens) and sports such as rugby or cricket.

- **Immigration and ethnic minorities:**
  After the Second World War and the end of the British Empire, lots of people from the former colonies **immigrated** to Britain to find work there. Most of them came from Asia (mainly India, Pakistan and Bangladesh), the Caribbean and Africa. In the following decades, Britain repeatedly restricted its immigration laws. Today, about 13 per cent of the British population belong to an **ethnic minority group**. Ever since their arrival, there have been discussions (both within the minority groups themselves and in the larger society) whether they

should keep their cultural traditions or rather adapt to a British lifestyle. Although most members of ethnic minorities are well-integrated, they still sometimes face discrimination, for example on the job market or in housing. Unfortunately, in recent years, prejudices and hate crimes against ethnic minority groups have increased, especially against people of Muslim faith.

- **Britain's relationship with the EU:**

  Britain's relationship with the EU has been quite complicated. Britain joined the EEC in 1973 – however, just two years later, the first referendum was held about whether or not the UK should really stay in the EEC. Although a majority voted "yes" at the time, a lot of Britons never really identified with Europe. Many had the impression that the UK paid more to the EU than it got back or were worried that the European influence would grow too strong. **Euroscepticism** increased dramatically when more and more immigrants from Eastern Europe came to the UK in the early 2000s. In the European elections in 2014, the right-wing UK Independence Party won the most votes. It exploited people's fear of immigration and xenophobic prejudices and created a strongly anti-EU climate. In 2016, a referendum was held in which a very small majority of the British population voted in favour of leaving the European Union. On 31 January 2020, the UK formally ended its EU membership, and in 2021, the new "Trade and Cooperation Agreement" *(Handels- und Kooperationsabkommen)* between the UK and the European Union came into effect.
  So far, the economic consequences of Brexit do not look good for the UK: According to a report from 2022, for example, the UK economy was doing worse than the other G7 countries (the largest so-called "advanced" economies: UK, USA, France, Germany, Italy, Japan, Canada).
  Interestingly, the majority of young Britons had voted to remain in the EU and is not happy at all about Brexit. In some parts of the UK, such as Scotland or Northern Ireland, the majority of people would also have liked to remain in the EU. As a result, the wish to become independent from the UK might become stronger in these countries (however, in 2022, the Supreme Court decided that the Scottish Parliament won't be allowed to hold a referendum about independence without the consent of the UK Parliament in London).

- **Education system:**
  British children have to attend school from the ages of 5 to 16. From 5 to 11, they attend primary school, later they go on to secondary school. Most pupils attend a **comprehensive school** which is open for pupils of all abilities. In some

areas, however, there are also grammar schools and secondary modern schools. About 93 per cent of pupils go to a **state school**, which is free of charge; about 7 per cent attend an **independent** or **private school**, for which you have to pay a fee. The so-called **public schools**, such as Eton or Harrow, are the most expensive private schools and are usually attended by children from very wealthy families. At the age of 16, pupils take their **GCSEs** (which is roughly equivalent to the *Mittlerer Schulabschluss*). After that, they can decide whether they want to leave school, pursue further education that prepares them for the job market, or stay on and do their **A-levels** (roughly equivalent to the *Abitur*). Those who want to study at university have to pay very high tuition fees *(Studiengebühren)* – often more than £ 9000 per year. As a result, people from poorer families often can't afford to go to a top university or fall into huge debt to do so.

- **Teens and young adults:**
  Teens in the UK enjoy most of the things teens in other countries do: They like to spend time on social media or playing online games, hanging out with friends, listening to music, playing sports, etc. Topics such as love, friendships, school pressure or worries about one's appearance are also concerns they share with teens elsewhere. Just like in other countries, lots of young people in Britain are worried about the effects of climate change. An increasing number of adolescents and young adults also fear that British society might become less tolerant after "Brexit".

Bildnachweis:
Karte Vereinigtes Königreich © NordNordWest, lizenziert nach CC BY-SA 3.0; Entwicklung des Union Jack: gemeinfrei; geteilte Flagge UK/EU © Tim Reckmann, lizenziert nach CC BY 2.0; Schüler*innen © michaeljung / shutterstock

Some aspects about New Zealand

New Zealand is an island country in the southwest of the Pacific Ocean, about 1,600 kilometres southeast of Australia.
It can be divided into two islands, the **North Island** and the **South Island**. These are sometimes referred to as "mainland" New Zealand. Apart from the two large islands there are **more than 700 smaller islands** which also belong to New Zealand.

- **Population and major cities:**
  Although New Zealand is slightly larger than the United Kingdom, only about 5 million people live there (compared to about 67 million in the UK).
  By far the most populous city in New Zealand is **Auckland**. New Zealand's capital city, however, is **Wellington**. Both cities are located on the North Island. **Christchurch** is the largest city on the South Island. The city suffered two severe earthquakes in September 2010 and February 2011. Thousands of buildings collapsed or were badly damaged, many people lost their lives. In 2019 Christchurch was the centre of a terrorist attack by a far-right extremist in which 51 people were killed. New Zealand's prime minister at that time described this tragedy as one of the darkest days in New Zealand's history.

- **Geography:**
  New Zealand is famous for its varied and spectacular landscapes. You can find long, **sandy beaches**, among which the Ninety Mile Beach is probably the most famous. The centre of the North Island is dominated by a **volcanic plateau**. The South Island is marked by the **Southern Alps**, a mountain range with many peaks more than 3,000 meters high. But New Zealand also has rain forests, fjords, glaciers, and much more. Peter Jackson's trilogy *Lord of the Rings* and *The Hobbit* were filmed in New Zealand and have made its stunning scenery more popular than ever before.

- **Plants and animals:**
  Because of its remote geographical position, there are many **endemic plants and animals** in New Zealand (which means they do not exist anywhere else in the world). The giant **kauri trees**, for example, are among the largest and oldest trees in the world. New Zealand is also famous for its birds, several of which are unable to fly. The most prominent example is the **kiwi**. It is a national symbol and in colloquial language New Zealanders are also often referred to as "kiwis". Other animals that can only be found in New Zealand are particular kinds of penguins, dolphins, sea lions and bats.

- **Key events in history:**
  New Zealand is very far off. This is why it had been unpopulated for a very long time. At the end of the 13th century the **Polynesians** started to settle in the country. They were the ones to develop the traditional **Māori culture**. The first European to catch sight of New Zealand was the Dutch **Abel Tasman** in 1642. When his ship reached Golden Bay, a bloody encounter with the Māori came about, probably because of a misunderstanding. Four Dutch sailors were killed and Abel Tasman ended up never even setting foot on the island. It was not until 1769 that a new expedition arrived at the New Zealand coast, this time under the leadership of **James Cook**, a captain of the British Royal Navy. Cook made maps of New Zealand and for a long time, he was celebrated by many (mainly white) New Zealanders as an ancestor-like figure. In recent years, he has come to be seen in a more critical light. During the first encounter with the Māori, Cook's men killed at least nine indigenous people – a traumatic experience for the Māori.

Statue of Kupe (Polynesian explorer who, according to some Māori narratives, discovered New Zealand)

After Cook, whale catchers, seal hunters and missionaries arrived in New Zealand, and the Māori and the European settlers began to exchange goods and

establish **trading relations**. Because of the fact that firearms were traded, violent disorders became more frequent. In the first half of the 19th century, several Māori tribes fought each other in the so-called **Musket Wars**, in which more than 20,000 people were killed. The white settlers also brought new **diseases**, such as measles *(Masern)*, and as a result many Māori died.
In 1840, the British and the Māori signed the **Treaty of Waitangi**. It is regarded as the founding document of New Zealand. The contract attached New Zealand to the British Crown and declared British sovereignty over the islands. Many Māori leaders signed the contract because they hoped that this would protect them against the French, who also had plans to colonise New Zealand. Moreover, the Māori leaders had been reassured by the British that they would keep ownership of their land and get the same rights as British subjects. However, as some parts of the treaty text were not translated accurately into Māori, there have been different interpretations of the contract. In the following years, a series of battles over land issues followed between government forces on the one hand and the Māori on the other. These are called the **New Zealand Wars (1845–1872)**. A lot of Māori unjustly **lost their land** to the British, which has been a source of pain ever since and can be seen as one of the reasons for the higher rate of poverty among the Māori.
In 1841, New Zealand became a **colony within the British Empire**. With the New Zealand Constitution Act in 1852 the country started to govern itself rather autonomously. Shortly afterwards, male Māori also got the right to vote and were able to have seats in parliament, and in the 1890s, New Zealand became the first country in the world to allow women to vote. In **1947** New Zealand finally gained **independence**. In the 1970s, a **Māori protest movement** was formed and the so-called **Waitangi Tribunal** was established, which allows Māori to complain about breaches against the treaty of Waitangi and claim compensation for their lost land.

- **Political system:**
  New Zealand is part of the Commonwealth of Nations and the British monarch is still the official head of state. New Zealand has a parliament and a cabinet, which is led by the prime minister.

- **Demographics and religion:**
  Today, about 70 per cent of New Zealanders are of European descent (in the Māori language they are called *Pākehā*), over 16 per cent are Māori, 15 per cent are Asian and 9 per cent Pacific Islanders. More than a quarter of New Zealanders were born outside the country. Nearly half of the population do not have a religion; about 37 per cent identify as Christians.

- **Economy:**
  The economy in New Zealand has always relied to a large extent on **agriculture**. New Zealand is the biggest exporter of sheep meat and dairy products, for example. However, other sectors, such as **tourism**, also play an increasingly important role. The currency used is the New Zealand dollar.

- **Culture:**
  New Zealand's culture is marked mainly by its **Māori and European heritage** as well as by cultural influences from other ethnic groups. Although most people speak English, about four per cent of the population also speak the Māori language *(Te Reo Māori)*. Further examples of Māori culture are its legends, artful tattoos, creative arts (such as weaving and carving), ritual dances (such as the *haka*) and many other customs (such as the *hongi*, a form of greeting by two people pressing their noses together).

- **Free time activities:**
  Sports are of great importance in New Zealand. **Rugby** is the national sport and New Zealand's national team, the "All Blacks", are known around the world. **Cricket** is also very popular and further testifies to the British influence on the country. New Zealand is also one of the leading nations at sailing. Other widespread free time activities are netball, water sports, golf, tennis, skiing/snowboarding as well as extreme sports, such as **bungee jumping**.

greeting each other with a *hongi*

Māori women's rugby team performing a *haka*

Bildnachweis:
Karte Neuseeland © danceyourlife/Shutterstock.com; Kauri-Baum © W. Bulach, lizenziert nach CC BY-SA 4.0; Kupe-Statue © Mike, lizenziert nach CC BY-SA 2.0; Hongi © Tim Rooke/Shutterstock.com; Haka © DANIEL POCKETT / EPA-EFE / Shutterstock.com

ÜBUNGSAUFGABEN

Hörverstehen

Du wirst in der ZP 10 mit zwei Aufgaben zu zwei unterschiedlichen Texten (und Themen) konfrontiert. Die **Textgrundlagen** können sehr vielfältig sein, z. B. ein Interview, ein Radiobericht, eine Szene aus einem Hörspiel, Nachrichten, ein Telefonat oder eine Rede.

Ablauf des Prüfungsteils Hörverstehen

Zunächst hast du Zeit, die Hintergrundinformationen und die Aufgabenstellung zu studieren. Beide Hörtexte sind ca. vier Minuten lang und werden dir (jeweils mit einer kleinen Pause dazwischen) nacheinander zweimal vorgespielt.

Im **ersten Teil** hörst du in der Regel einen Hörtext mit einer sprechenden Person (**monologisches Sprechen**), im **zweiten Teil** aller Voraussicht nach eine Art Gespräch zwischen Personen (**dialogisches Sprechen**).

Häufige Aufgabenformate

Beim Hörverstehen sollst du den Texten Hauptinformationen, Gesamtaussagen und wichtige Details entnehmen. Außerdem musst du wesentliche Einstellungen der Sprechenden identifizieren.

Es gibt mehrere mögliche **Aufgabentypen**, die wir dir in diesem Kapitel kurz vorstellen. Die einzelnen Aufgaben werden in der Reihenfolge immer chronologisch zum Hörverlauf angeordnet – außer beim *Matching* (s. u.).
In den letzten Prüfungen kamen in erster Linie *Multiple-Choice*-Aufgaben vor.

Beispieltext: Interview with a student about debate clubs at British schools

Transcript:

(1) **Journalist:** In British schools, students can join various clubs offering interesting activities. These include debating clubs, for example. What is unique about them?

Student: By practising debating, students develop competencies like critical reading and doing thorough research in preparation as well as evidence-based, sophisticated argumentation in lively debates with interesting people.

(2) **Journalist:** That sounds great. What kinds of conflicts or problems do you usually discuss in competitions?

Student: That varies a lot. You become proficient in discussing relevant questions relating to political issues, environmental challenges, globalisation, culture and legislation, for example.

(3) **Journalist:** What would you say the benefit is for you personally for your career after you leave school?

Student: I guess you profit from the debates by gaining self-confidence and by learning to present yourself naturally in professional situations, which could be useful in the future.

Multiple Choice

Du musst aus drei Antwortmöglichkeiten eine inhaltlich passende Aussage zu einem Hörtext auswählen. Eine Schwierigkeit ist dabei, dass meist alle drei Optionen einen gewissen Sinn ergeben, es gibt aber nur eine richtige Lösung. Der Wortlaut der Antworten ist in der Regel nicht mit dem Wortlaut der Hörtexte identisch. Eine weitere „Falle“ kann sein, dass zwar Phrasen aus dem Text vorkommen, dass aber die inhaltliche Aussage nicht exakt zum Text passt.

Beispielaufgabe und Musterlösung:

In debate clubs, students learn to …

a) ☑ argue reasonably.

b) ☐ convince others of their opinion.

c) ☐ attack debaters cleverly.

Filling in the Gaps/Short Answers

Du bist z. B. aufgefordert, einen Satzanfang mit einer Aussage zum Hörtext sinnvoll zu vervollständigen.
Alternative Antwortmöglichkeiten sind in der Musterlösung immer mit einem Schrägstrich abgetrennt.

Beispielaufgabe und Musterlösung:

Not only do students learn how to debate, but they also learn how to think/read critically / learn how to research a topic in detail.

Eine ähnliche Aufgabe ist, dass du eine inhaltlich passende Kurzantwort zu einer Frage zum Hörtext formulieren oder aber Beispiele anführen sollst. In der Musterlösung sind alle denkbaren Antworten aufgelistet. Halte dich aber in deiner Prüfung genau an Vorgaben wie "Give three examples".

Beispielaufgabe und Musterlösung:

Give three examples of discussion categories in debates:

- political problems / environmental issues
- globalisation / cultural trends
- issues concerning legislation

Matching

Diese Art von Aufgabe ist möglich, kam aber bisher nicht vor. Denkbar wäre, dass du z. B. mehreren Kurztexten oder Textabschnitten jeweils eine Überschrift zuordnen sollst. Oft gibt es mehr Überschriften als Hörpassagen.

Beispielaufgabe und Musterlösung:

Match the following headings (A–D) with the correct section of the text (1–3). There is one more heading than you need:

A Debating rules
B Character building
C Skill focus
D Range of topics

Section	1	2	3
Heading	C	D	B

Strategien im Bereich Hörverstehen

Vorbereitung im Schullalltag

Auf diese Aufgaben kannst du dich grundsätzlich vorbereiten, indem du z. B.

- die Vokabeln deines Lehrbuchs und/oder anderer Materialien aus dem Unterricht regelmäßig lernst und somit Inhalte schneller verstehst.
- regelmäßig englischsprachige Hörtexte bzw. Videos (z. B. Podcasts, *tutorials, documentaries, news/music programmes, interviews*) hörst oder anschaust.

Durch das Schauen von Filmen und Serien in englischer Sprache (ggf. zuerst mit englischsprachigen Untertiteln, dann ohne) kannst du am bequemsten dein Ohr für die Fremdsprache und ihr Verstehen trainieren. Nutze die Übungen in diesem Buch und versuche, diese nach und nach wie in der Prüfung zu bearbeiten. Zu Beginn kannst du die Hörtexte ggf. auch häufiger als zweimal anhören oder zwischendurch pausieren. Kontrolliere die Lösungen erst nach der vollständigen Bearbeitung und lies nur im Transkript (vgl. Lösungsteil) nach, wenn du einen gesprochenen Text auch nach mehrfachem Hören nicht verstehst.

Tipps für die Bewältigung der Aufgaben

Vor dem ersten Hören:

- Kläre zunächst für dich, welche **Art von Hörtext** vorliegt (Rede, Interview, …?) und wer spricht.
- Mach dir schnell anhand der Überschrift und/oder Einleitung bewusst, was das **Thema** ist und welche **Bezugskultur** im Fokus steht.
- Lies nun zügig, aber genau die Aufgaben und ggf. weitere Hinweise.

Während des ersten und zweiten Hörens:

- Folge konzentriert den Aussagen. Versuche beim ersten Zuhören bereits Aufgaben zu beantworten.
- Mach dir keine Sorgen, wenn du nicht jedes Wort verstehst. Das ist nicht schlimm und vollkommen natürlich als Nicht-Muttersprachler*in. Viele unbekannte Wörter kannst du aus dem Zusammenhang erschließen, außerdem gibt es auch gar nicht zu jeder Textstelle eine Frage.
- Nutze die kurze Pause nach dem ersten Hören: Kontrolliere deine Antworten, versuche noch offene Fragen zu beantworten und markiere, auf welche Aufgaben du dich beim zweiten Hören besonders konzentrieren solltest. Da die Aufgaben chronologisch angeordnet sind, kannst du abschätzen, an welcher Stelle du besonders gut aufpassen musst.
- Ärgere dich nicht, wenn du eine Aufgabe nicht lösen kannst.

Listening Test 1

(gesellschaftliches Engagement, Berufsorientierung)

In dieser Übung trainierst du das Multiple-Choice-*Format.*

Text — Michelle Obama: "Who are you gonna be?"

Michelle Obama is a US lawyer and author. She is married to Barack Obama and served as First Lady from 2009 to 2017 when Barack Obama was the first African American President of the United States. In her role as First Lady Michelle Obama held a **speech** in front of Eastern Kentucky University's Class of 2013.

- *First read the annotations and the tasks.*
- *Then listen to the extract.*
- *While you are listening, tick the correct box.*
- *At the end you will hear the extract again.*
- *Now read the tasks. You have **90 seconds** to do this.*
- *Now listen to the extract and do the tasks.*

Annotations

conscientiousness – concentration and effort
West Point cadet – student at US Military Academy 'West Point'
grit – firmness of character, courage
EKU – **E**astern **K**entucky **U**niversity
veteran – ex-military, e. g. US soldier who has served in a war

Tasks

Tick (✓) the correct answer.

1. Michelle Obama asks what you will do when you are …
   a) ☐ a successful teacher.
   b) ☐ facing challenges at work.
   c) ☐ criticised by an employer.

2. The situations that shape us are characterised by …
   a) ☐ failure.
   b) ☐ hardship.
   c) ☐ regret.

3. For success, mental strength and effort are …
   a) ☐ more relevant than intelligence.
   b) ☐ less relevant than good grades in exams.
   c) ☐ just as relevant as intelligence or good grades.

4. Ambition helped military students to …
   a) ☐ deal with challenges.
   b) ☐ spot and avoid mistakes.
   c) ☐ become role models of strength.

5. Learning from mistakes is …
   a) ☐ a key to overcoming problems.
   b) ☐ particularly difficult.
   c) ☐ not regarded highly.

6. At Eastern Kentucky University students …
   a) ☐ had to do charity work.
   b) ☐ gave money to a local newspaper.
   c) ☐ went on a trip to support victims of a storm.

7. Former US soldiers …
   a) ☐ offer classes to the students at EKU.
   b) ☐ were recently honored by President Obama.
   c) ☐ are included in campus life.

8. For students at EKU military experience …
   a) ☐ is a necessity.
   b) ☐ can mean extra credit.
   c) ☐ has been written about in a magazine.

9. Michelle Obama hopes that after university students will …
   a) ☐ pursue a career in the military.
   b) ☐ be involved in helping society.
   c) ☐ profit personally from volunteering.

Lösungsvorschläge

Transcript Michelle Obama: "Who are you gonna be?"

And my first question is: Who are you gonna be? And if you'll notice, I'm not asking what are you gonna do, but who are you gonna be? I'm asking you about how you plan to live your life every day. How are you gonna respond when you don't get that job you had your heart set on?

For all of you who are going on to be teachers, what are you gonna do if the students in your class next year just don't respond to your lessons? For all of you going into business, how will you react when your boss gives you a goal that feels way too high?

See, these are the moments that define us – not the day you get the promotion, not the day you win teacher of the year, but the times that force you to claw and scratch and fight just to get through the day; the moments when you get knocked down and you're wondering whether it's even worth it to get back up. See, those are the times when you've got to ask yourself, who am I gonna be?

And I want to be clear, this isn't just some vague platitude about building character. In recent years, we've actually been seeing a growing body of research that shows that skills like resilience and conscientiousness can be just as important to your success as your test scores, or even your IQ.

For instance, West Point cadets who scored high on things like grit and determination were more likely to complete basic training than those who ranked high on things like class rank, SAT scores, and physical fitness. So, what we're seeing is that if you're willing to dig deep, if you're willing to pick yourself up when you fall, if you're willing to work and work until your weaknesses become your strengths, then you'll develop a set of skills that you can mold and apply to any situation you encounter, any job you might have, any crisis you might confront.

But you've got to make that choice – who are you gonna be? And then once you answered that question, I want you to answer a second question, and that is: How are you gonna take those skills and experiences that you've gained and use them to serve others?

See, here at Eastern, you have an extraordinary culture of service. Many of you spent your spring break volunteering in places like New Orleans and Washington, D.C. Your journalism society donated all the money they'd raised for a trip to a regional conference to a newspaper that had been hit by a tornado.

Altogether, EKU students volunteered 107,000 hours of service, earning you a place on my husband the President's Higher Education Community Service Honor Roll. *(Applause.)* Absolutely. Absolutely. And on top of all of that, you have also given back to our country by opening your arms and welcoming our nation's veterans into your community. And everyone here is involved in that – everyone. *(Applause.)*

The administration awards college credit for military experience. Faculty members reach out to veterans in their classrooms. Students donate to the veterans' book exchange every semester. So, it is no wonder that two out of the last three years, Military Times EDGE magazine has named you the nation's number one four-year school for our veterans. *(Applause.)* So you all should be very proud of this community.

But graduates, graduates, you can't stop serving once you leave here. Whether you've worn our country's uniform or not, we're all called to serve and to give back to those around us. And you don't have to travel across the globe or even across the country to find ways to serve. All you have to do is take a look around your own community.

Are there kids in your neighborhood who could use a mentor? Can you volunteer with an organization that serves military families? Can you pick up a few extra cans of vegetables and donate them to a food bank? I mean, these things may seem so small, but they really make a difference. Because when you've worked hard and done well, as I said, the least you can do is reach back and give a hand to somebody else who could use that help. *(Applause.)*

From: https://obamawhitehouse.archives.gov/the-press-office/2013/05/11/remarks-first-lady-eastern-kentucky-university-commencement

HINT

In folgenden Textstellen des Transkripts findest du jeweils die Lösungen:

1 "How are you gonna respond when you don't get that job you had your heart set on? […] what are you gonna do if the students in your class next year just don't respond to your lessons? […] how will you react when your boss gives you a goal that feels way too high?" (ll. 3–8)

2 "These are the moments that define us […] the times that force you to claw and scratch and fight just to get through the day; the moments when you get knocked down and you're wondering whether it's even worth it to get back up." (ll. 9–12)

3 "skills like resilience and conscientiousness can be just as important to your success as your test scores, or even your IQ." (ll. 16/17)

4 "For instance, West Point cadets who scored high on things like grit and determination were more likely to complete basic training than those who ranked high on things like class rank, SAT scores, and physical fitness." (ll. 18–20)

5 "if you're willing to pick yourself up when you fall, if you're willing to work and work until your weaknesses become your strengths, then you'll develop a set of skills that you can mold and apply to any situation you encounter, any job you might have, any crisis you might confront." (ll. 21–24)

6 "Your journalism society donated all the money they'd raised for a trip to a regional conference to a newspaper that had been hit by a tornado." (ll. 31/32)

7 "you have also given back to our country by opening your arms and welcoming our nation's veterans into your community." (ll. 35–37)

8 "The administration awards college credit for military experience." (l. 39)

9 "Can you volunteer with an organization that serves military families? Can you pick up a few extra cans of vegetables and donate them to a food bank? [...] the least you can do is reach back and give a hand to somebody else who could use that help." (ll. 50–55)

1. Michelle Obama asks what you will do when you are …

   b) ☑ facing challenges at work.

2. The situations that shape us are characterised by …

   b) ☑ hardship.

3. For success, mental strength and effort are …

   c) ☑ just as relevant as intelligence or good grades.

4. Ambition helped military students to …

   a) ☑ deal with challenges.

5. Learning from mistakes is …

   a) ☑ a key to overcoming problems.

6. At Eastern Kentucky University students …

   b) ☑ gave money to a local newspaper.

7. Former US soldiers …

   c) ☑ are included in campus life.

8. For students at EKU military experience …

   b) ☑ can mean extra credit.

9. Michelle Obama hopes that after university students will …

   b) ☑ be involved in helping society.

Listening Test 2
(kulturelle, soziale, politische Aspekte; Demokratie und Menschenrechte)

■ *In dieser Übung trainierst du das* Matching-*Format und das Verstehen von Gesamtaussagen von einzelnen britischen Persönlichkeiten zu einem Thema.*

Text **Women, power and politics in the UK**

For a report about the role of women in politics the British Council, the UK organisation for cultural relations and educational opportunities, asked many people, such as politicians, academics and activists, about their opinions and their experiences.

- *First read the annotations and the tasks.*
- *Then listen to the extract.*
- *While you are listening, match each person with the right statement.*
- *At the end you will hear the extract again.*
- *Now read the tasks. You have* ***90 seconds*** *to do this.*
- *Now listen to the extract and do the tasks.*

Annotations
P4s, P5s – terms for school year groups in Scottish primary schools
BME background – expression to refer to people from **B**lack and **m**inority **e**thnic groups
intersectionality – system to explain how different categories (e. g. race, gender, religion) are connected and cause discrimination and/or privilege
quota – here: *Frauenquote*

Task

You will hear seven people addressing a certain aspect related to the topic in chronological order (1–7). Who says what? **Match** the statements below (A–I) with the correct person. Choose the best statement for each person. There are two more statements than you need.

1 Mikalya Jones
2 Maria Miller
3 Mike Nesbitt
4 Ruth Boyle
5 Harriet Andrews
6 Laura McAllister
7 Bethany Young

A Let's create awareness for gender equality among students.
B It is not enough to have more female MPs. We need women who represent the richness of our culture.
C In education today we need to have more reflection on identity.
D An inclusive society should also be reflected in politics and in who has a say.
E Men sometimes prevent women from pursuing a career.
F Women should take more responsibility and shape the world.
G Women still need to argue their cause and should form a strong and inclusive community.
H Women should be paid more money in low-income jobs.
I I hope for more female politicians.

HINT Be careful, there are two more statements than necessary. Some statements seem to apply to more than one person. Concentrate on those when you listen for the second time to make the best choice.

Person	1	2	3	4	5	6	7
Statement							

Lösungsvorschläge

Transcript — Women, power and politics in the UK

1 Mikalya Jones: I'd like to see women and girls more confident in making decisions that affect them and people around them. So whether that's about mentoring, whether that's around accessing the space and just being more comfortable in that arena so that they can be the ones to make the decisions for them and the rest of the world.

2 Rt Hon Maria Miller: What I want to see happen in Parliament is that we have 50% of our members of Parliament are women. An equal parliament in ten years' time is the very least we can expect 100 years on from women first getting the vote.

3 Mike Nesbitt: Gender equality is a massive issue, but clearly it's not being treated with the due concern that it deserves. And I sense the frustration of the delegates here today. There are many actions that can be taken, but it must be tackled strategically. And I would like to see a ten-year programme within our schools remembering that today's P4s and P5s will be the voters in ten years' time and they can go to the polls with an entirely different attitude.

4 Ruth Boyle: I think over the next ten years, I'd like to see continued progress towards equality. So we want to make sure that we're defending the gains that we've already made. And I think the way we build on that progress is through quotas and for representation in Parliament. And I think without that, we're not going to be able to make the final leap in towards genuine equality. And I think as well, I'd like to see a more diverse group of women in the Parliament. So thinking about younger women, women from BME backgrounds, disabled women and also women from LGBT, and I think then we'll really have a wealth of voices in Parliament. That means we'll have better legislation, a more representative Parliament, and probably that will encourage more people to get involved in politics in the future. So I think everyone would benefit from that.

5 Harriet Andrews: I would like to see conversations about gender being routine in schools and opportunities for both boys and girls to explore their gender and how a gendered society affects them. And because I think only by having these conversations will we move forward the culture in the UK.

6 Laura McAllister: I think the change I'd like to see, there's a whole range of choices, of course, but the biggest change I'd like to see would be that women rediscover their voices again. I'm very worried about the current state of feminism. I think there's been a backlash to the whole feminist movement, which has put women off declaring themselves to be feminists. And I think a lot of men as well feel that women have achieved almost everything with regard to equality. So I'd like to see that be recalibrated as a movement that appeals to the whole variety of women's identities across classes, across ages, across intersectionality, all of those different aspects. And I think that would act as a sounding board for us to campaign for the next generation of important equality interventions. And they really relate to everything from reproductive rights to closing the gender pay gap, to getting women in powerful positions in politics and public life. But I think without a campaigning voice, we'll struggle to keep the momentum up on all of those things.

7 **Bethany Young:** I would like to see a higher representation of disabled women in politics and a greater level of inclusion in decision making in general.

From: https://www.britishcouncil.org/society/womens-and-girls-empowerment/women-power-politics-whats-changed

HINT

Auch wenn hier auf den ersten Blick mehrere Überschriften auf eine Aussage zutreffend erscheinen mögen, gibt es immer eine Aussage, die in besonderer Hinsicht zutrifft. Dies kannst du ggf. im Transkript nachvollziehen:

1–F: Mikalya Jones fächert verschiedene Arbeitsfelder für Frauen auf und betont die weltweite Tragweite, die Frauen durch ihre Tätigkeiten in diesen Feldern erreichen: "they can be the ones to make the decisions for them and the rest of the world" (Z. 4/5)

2–I: Diese Aussage trifft grundsätzlich auf mehrere Personen zu, allerdings fokussiert Maria Miller als einzige diesen Aspekt im Bereich der Politik (vgl. Z. 6/7).

3–A: Hier passt auf den ersten Blick auch C; A ist aber treffender, denn Mike Nesbitt betont als einziger die Notwendigkeit, **Gleichberechtigung** in einem frühen Lebensstadium bewusst zu machen (vgl. Z. 13/14).

4–B, 7–D: Ruth Boyle (4) und Bethany Young (7) haben ähnliche Ansichten, allerdings schlägt Ruth Boyle einen breiteren diversen Bogen (vgl. Z. 21–24), wohingegen Bethany Young sich v. a. mehr Beteiligung von Frauen mit einer Behinderung in der Politik und generell bei wichtigen Entscheidungen wünscht (vgl. Z. 45/46).

5–C: Harriet Andrews fokussiert nicht wie Mike Nesbitt (3) die Gleichberechtigung, sondern die grundsätzliche Thematisierung von Geschlechtsidentität im Unterricht (vgl. Z. 27–29).

6–G: Laura McAllister betont die Notwendigkeit, die Frauenbewegung von damals neu zu denken.

7–D: vgl. oben

Person	1	2	3	4	5	6	7
Statement	F	I	A	B	C	G	D

Listening Test 3

(Jugendkulturen, Migration und Mobilität in der globalisierten Welt)

▪ *In dieser Übung trainierst du das* Filling in the Gaps/Short Answers-*Format und vor allem das Filtern nach spezifischen Details.*

Text **The benefits of taking a gap year**

The following podcast is about gap year experiences in Israel. In the excerpt, you will first listen to a conversation between the two hosts, Margo Brookfield and Julia Rogers, and then to Julia's interview with a young gapper called Ayden Novick.

- *First read the annotations and the tasks.*
- *Then listen to the extract.*
- *While you are listening, note down the correct answers in keywords.*
- *At the end you will hear the extract again.*
- *Now read the tasks. You have* **90 seconds** *to do this.*
- *Now listen to the extract and do the tasks.*

Annotations

gap year – *ein freies Jahr (in der Regel zwischen Schule und Studium)*
gapper – a person taking a gap year
alum – former *(ehemalig)* member of an organisation or programme
kibbutz – a collective, spiritual community in Israel that was traditionally based on agriculture

Tasks

1. **Fill in** the correct information:

   a) At the beginning of the show, the hosts ______________________.

   b) In her professional life, Phyllis Folb is ______________________.

   c) Margo also knows Phyllis Folb because they have ______________________ amongst the members of their association.

   d) Phyllis Folb's book *Find your right direction* is a ______________________ ______________________.

2. **Give examples** from the text in short answers:

a) Give **five** different examples of program options in Israel.

- ______________________________
- ______________________________
- ______________________________
- ______________________________
- ______________________________

b) Give **three** examples of why Israel is a diverse country according to Julia.

- ______________________________
- ______________________________
- ______________________________

c) Give **two** reasons why Ayden Novick decided to take a gap year.

- ______________________________
- ______________________________

d) Name **two** goals of the BBYO organisation.

- ______________________________
- ______________________________

Transcript The benefits of taking a gap year

Margo Brookfield: Hello Gap Year universe, I'm Margo Brookfield.

Julia Rogers: And I'm Julia Rogers. Welcome to Gap Year Radio, the show that brings you information and inspiration to plan a life-changing gap year adventure.

Margo Brookfield: So, Julia, today we are welcoming two guests who will describe the different types of gap year experiences that you can have in Israel. So, I know that you had two really engaging conversations, Julia, and obviously there are so many options and programs in Israel, so who exactly did you speak with?

Julia Rogers: Yeah, I had some really fun conversations, so I spoke with Ayden Novick, who is a gap year alum, and he spent his gap year with the program "Young Judea", which the gappers spend half their time in Tel Aviv and half their time in Jerusalem over the course of a full year. It's a full-year program. And then I also had a chance to speak with a friend of the pod and friend of the gap year industry, Phyllis Folb, who is the executive director of the American Israel Gap Year Association. So, she literally wrote the book on gap years in Israel, and we talk about that book in our interview.

Margo Brookfield: Oh my gosh, yes, Phyllis I've certainly seen at the gap year circuit, on the many Zoom calls that we have every week amongst the Gap Year Association members and programs and such. So how awesome that she was able to share her many years of experience with you.

Julia Rogers: Yeah, she really has built her career on understanding the different types of gap year experiences you can have in Israel, which are … way more variety than even I thought there were. You know, I learned new things through our discussion and through her book as well, which is called *Find your right direction*, and so, it's actually a guide to gap year programs in Israel. So, if anybody wants to understand the breadth of options, you can actually get her book.

Margo Brookfield: Amazing, and so Julia, I know you've mentioned this now and I am only just coming to recognize how many different program options there are in Israel. So, what are just some examples of the different types of program options? I know you'll go into it in more depth, but what are some of these options?

Julia Rogers: Yeah, well, you know, one of the cool things I think about programs in Israel is that they're almost like a microcosm of what we would think of as the greater gap year ecosystem of opportunities. So, there are surface learning programs, there are faith-based programs, there are secular programs, there are internship programs, there are tech start-up programs, there are, you know, farming programs and conservation programs and marine biology programs. Like, everything that you would think of as, like, kind of out there in the world for gappers, it seems like there's a version of that in Israel 'cause it's such a diverse country with, like, there being, like, these really large cities and then also these very ancient and holy, you know, religious sites, as well as this history of farming and kibbutz-living, which has kind of this more, you know, free spirit vibe to it. So it really runs a spectrum.

Margo Brookfield: Oh my gosh, amazing! Well, certainly a great option in terms of locations for students to look into, but I'm definitely excited to hear more about the many different types of gap experiences that that you're gonna discuss and tell us more about.

Julia Rogers: Well, wait no more! Let's get started.

Margo Brookfield: Thanks for listening.

(music)

Julia Rogers: Ayden, thank you so much for being here today, and I can't wait to hear your story.

Ayden Novick: Of course, thank you so much for having me. I'm really excited to be here.

Julia Rogers: Great! So, all right, let's start from the very beginning. Why did you decide to take a gap year?

Ayden Novick: Well, so I had a pretty standard high school experience. It was not boring but pretty uneventful. When I was thinking about the idea of college, I just wasn't exactly ready to do four more years of school. I wasn't exactly sure at that time what I was gonna do, but I just knew I didn't, I didn't want to go immediately to college. Along around my senior year, I think it was my … winter break of my senior year, a little bit after, I started to think about a gap year in Israel. And then around February of that year, when I was at an international convention for BBYO I talked to the Young Judea year course, like, booth that they had at the convention and I learned about the program.

Julia Rogers: Cool, and for those who don't know, what is BBYO?

Ayden Novick: BBYO is a … international Jewish youth leadership movement, so it's all about, like, connecting Jewish teens all across the world and learning more about Judaism while making new friends.

Julia Rogers: That sounds cool – so that was something you were pretty involved with in high school?

Ayden Novick: Yeah, it was a youth group that I was pretty involved with … *(fade out)*

From: http://gapyearradiopodcast.com/ep-602-gapping-in-israel-with-author-and-israel-gap-year-expert-phyllis-folb-and-alum-ayden-novick/

HINT

In folgenden Textstellen des Transkripts findest du jeweils die Lösungen:

1 **a** vgl. Z. 1–9

b "Phyllis Folb, who is the executive director of the American Israel Gap Year Association. […] she literally wrote the book on gap years in Israel" (Z. 14–16)

c "on the many Zoom calls that we have every week amongst the Gap Year Association members" (Z. 18/19)

d "it's actually a guide to gap year programs in Israel" (l. 25)

2 **a** "there are surface learning programs, there are faith-based programs, there are secular programs, there are internship programs, there are tech start-up programs, there are, you know, farming programs and conservation programs and marine biology programs." (ll. 35–38)

b "it's such a diverse country with, […] these really large cities […] these very ancient and holy […] religious sites, as well as this history of farming and kibbutz-living, which has […] free spirit vibe to it." (ll. 40–44)

c "I had a pretty standard high school experience […] but pretty uneventful. […] I just wasn't exactly ready to do four more years of school. I wasn't exactly sure at that time what I was gonna do, […] I didn't want to go immediately to college." (ll. 58–62)

d "so it's all about, like, connecting Jewish teens all across the world and learning more about Judaism while making new friends" (ll. 68–70)

1. a) At the beginning of the show, the hosts **introduce themselves / welcome/greet their audience/listeners / introduce the main topic / mention their guests / the people who have been interviewed**.

   b) In her professional life, Phyllis Folb is **an author/the executive director of a gap year association**.

   c) Margo also knows Phyllis Folb because they have **many Zoom/video calls** amongst the members of their association.

   d) Phyllis Folb's book *Find your right direction* is a **guide to gap year programs (in Israel)**.

2. a) *mögliche Lösungen (fünf Beispiele erforderlich):* surface learning programs, faith-based programs, secular programs, internships, tech start-up programs, farming programs, conservation programs, marine biology programs

   b) *mögliche Lösungen (drei Beispiele erforderlich):*
   - large cities
   - ancient/holy/historic sites/places

- history of farming
- history of kibbutz-living
- free spirit vibes

c) • uneventful life at high school
- didn't want to go directly to college /
  wasn't ready to go to school for four more years /
  wasn't sure what to do (right) after high school

d) • learning about Judaism
- connecting Jewish teens/young Jews from all over the world

Listening Test 4

(Wirtschaft & Technologie, Konsum, Berufsorientierung)

■ *In dieser Übung trainierst du das* Multiple-Choice-*Format. Es kommt besonders häufig in der Prüfung vor.*

Text **New Zealand students to build sporting equipment using plants**

The following podcast is based on a report from the "Voice of America" website: Two students from the University of Canterbury in New Zealand were interviewed about their studies and work at university.

- *First read the annotations and the tasks.*
- *Then listen to the extract.*
- *While you are listening, tick the correct box.*
- *At the end you will hear the extract again.*
- *Now read the tasks. You have **90 seconds** to do this.*
- *Now listen to the extract and do the tasks.*

Annotations
flax – kind of plant
carbon fiber – *Kohlenstofffaser (synthetische Faser)*
corn starch – *Maisstärke, Maismehl*
resin – *Harz*

Tasks

Tick (✓) the correct answer.

1. The students have created sustainable material made from …
   a) ☐ different trees.
   b) ☐ a tree and another plant.
   c) ☐ the cabbage tree only.

2. When produced, sustainable materials …
   a) ☐ don't harm the environment.
   b) ☐ are created for very long-term use.
   c) ☐ cause less ecological damage.

3. Outdoor equipment is commonly produced with …
   a) ☐ synthetic materials.
   b) ☐ natural materials.
   c) ☐ synthetic and natural materials.
4. The students from the University of Canterbury …
   a) ☐ believe in their own outdoor expertise.
   b) ☐ have used an innovative approach to design their product.
   c) ☐ have developed a skateboard made of non natural components.
5. Skateboards made of natural material …
   a) ☐ are as strong as fiberglass.
   b) ☐ are more likely to break.
   c) ☐ are stronger than the ones made of fiberglass.
6. The students want to develop outdoor items with fiber …
   a) ☐ that is a mixture of natural and non natural substances.
   b) ☐ taken from the leaves of a local tree.
   c) ☐ from a plant combined with other natural materials.
7. Potential professional partners …
   a) ☐ are curious about the experiment.
   b) ☐ are from New Zealand and other countries.
   c) ☐ want to build boats with the material.
8. The students …
   a) ☐ are thinking about forming their own start-up to sell the product.
   b) ☐ are being contacted by start-ups that produce outdoor equipment.
   c) ☐ may attract other industries.
9. The basic idea of using these natural resources …
   a) ☐ is appreciated by the Māori community in New Zealand.
   b) ☐ also relies on knowledge from the Māori culture.
   c) ☐ will now be adopted in New Zealand and Europe.

Lösungsvorschläge

Transcript New Zealand students to build sporting equipment using plants

Students from New Zealand have developed sustainable materials made from the leaves of a tree local to New Zealand, the cabbage tree, and a plant whose seeds are often eaten, flax.

Sustainable materials are products that are made in a way that limits their harm to the environment and the amount of resources they take. They support a long-term ecological balance.

The sustainable material the New Zealand students developed could soon be used to make high-performance outdoor sporting equipment like skis, kayaks, and skateboards. Their plan is to replace the traditional materials that are used like fiberglass and carbon fiber.

Skateboards, for instance, need to be particularly strong. Ben Scales and William Murrell are two students at New Zealand's University of Canterbury. They believe they can make them even stronger by using fiber from plants.

After experimenting in their at-home workshops, they created new, natural composite material, or material made up of different items.

Scales is 21 years old, studies product design and said their first attempt is looking good. He explained that their first experimental product is a skateboard that is made up of 25 percent fiber from a plant called harakeke and 75 percent recycled polylactic acid, which is plastic made from corn starch.

He added that the material is good to make a skateboard because it can take the force and shocks skateboards receive better than what skateboards are now made from: wood or carbon fiber.

The fiber is taken from the Harakeke plant: a native flax plant in New Zealand. The fiber is mixed with different resins, which is a product that comes from some trees that can be used to cover a surface or hold objects together. Leaves from the cabbage tree are also an important part of their material.

The plan is to use these sustainable materials to make skis, snowboards, and kayaks, as these outdoor sporting items are currently made from non natural materials like fiberglass and carbon fiber.

The university students have found interest from possible business partners in other countries.

Ben Scales told us some of the companies include businesses in Europe that make everything from boats to skis. Apart from that, a few overseas start-ups are interested in their work as they are currently trying to shape the personal transport industry. The student made clear that these start-ups are looking to use new sustainable materials that are just not offered in industries yet and they intend to use the students' material once they have gotten it ready, which will hopefully be soon.

If they are successful, the young Kiwi scientists could bring new life to New Zealand's flax fiber industry. They could also bring back practices used by the native people, the Māori, before European colonization.

Adapted from: https://learningenglish.voanews.com/a/new-zealand-students-to-build-high-performance-sporting-equipment-using-plants/5967304.html

HINT

In folgenden Textstellen des Transkripts findest du jeweils die Lösungen:

1 "materials made from the leaves of a tree local to New Zealand, the cabbage tree, and a plant whose seeds are often eaten, flax" (ll. 1–3)

2 "are made in a way that limits their harm to the environment and the amount of resources they take" (ll. 4/5)

3 "Their plan is to replace the traditional materials that are used like fiberglass and carbon fiber." (ll. 9/10)

4 "After experimenting in their at-home workshops, they created new, natural composite material, or material made up of different items" (ll. 14/15), "their first experimental product" (l. 17)

5 "the material is good to make a skateboard because it can take the force and shocks skateboards receive better than what skateboards are now made from: wood or carbon fiber" (ll. 20–22)

6 "The fiber is taken from the Harakeke plant: a native flax plant in New Zealand. The fiber is mixed with different resins, which is a product that comes from some trees that can be used to cover a surface or hold objects together. Leaves from the cabbage tree are also an important part of their material." (ll. 23–26); auch etwas weiter oben im Text befindet sich bereits eine passende Stelle: "made up of 25 percent fiber from a plant called harakeke and 75 percent recycled polylactic acid, which is plastic made from corn starch" (ll. 18/19)

7 "The university students have found interest from possible business partners in other countries." (ll. 30/31)

8 "Apart from that, a few overseas start-ups are interested in their work as they are currently trying to shape the personal transport industry. The student made clear that these start-ups are looking to use new sustainable materials that are just not offered in industries yet and they intend to use the students' material" (ll. 33–37)

9 "the young Kiwi scientists could bring new life to New Zealand's flax fiber industry. They could also bring back practices used by the native people, the Māori" (ll. 39–41)

1. The students have created sustainable material made from …

   b) ☑ a tree and another plant.

2. When produced, sustainable materials …

   c) ☑ cause less ecological damage.

3. Outdoor equipment is commonly produced with …

   a) ☑ synthetic materials.

4. The students from the University of Canterbury …

   b) ☑ have used an innovative approach to design their product.

5. Skateboards made of natural material …

   c) ☑ are stronger than the ones made of fiberglass.

6. The students want to develop outdoor items with fiber …

   c) ☑ from a plant combined with other natural materials.

7. Potential professional partners …

   a) ☑ are curious about the experiment.

8. The students …

   c) ☑ may attract other industries.

9. The basic idea of using these natural resources …

   b) ☑ also relies on knowledge from the Māori culture.

Leseverstehen

Es gibt viele verschiedene Arten von Lesetexten, z. B. Zeitungsartikel, Blog-Einträge, Romanauszüge und viele mehr. Ebenso vielfältig können die Aufgabenstellungen dazu sein. Viele kennst du sicher gut aus dem Englischunterricht. Welche Texte und Aufgaben dich in der zentralen Prüfung erwarten und wie du dich darauf am besten vorbereitest, erfährst du in diesem Kapitel.

Häufige Aufgabenformate

Beim Leseverstehen gibt es mehrere mögliche **Aufgabentypen**. Besonders häufig kam in den Prüfungen der letzten Jahre eine Kombination aus *Multiple-Choice-* und *True-False*-Aufgaben vor. Wir stellen dir hier aber noch weitere mögliche Aufgabentypen vor.

Für die allermeisten Aufgaben gilt: Die Teilaufgaben werden in der Reihenfolge immer chronologisch zum Textverlauf angeordnet (eine Ausnahme ist *Matching*).

Beispieltext:

(1) More and more Europeans are affected by the climate crisis and discuss ideas for fighting global warming.

(2) Sometimes, young people protest in a rather crass manner to create awareness for the global issue and their concerns. They organise sit-ins in public places (e. g. they block intersections, causing traffic jams) or use mashed potatoes to smear famous paintings protected by bullet-proof glass in museums.

(3) The majority of citizens can relate to their cause but do not approve of the measures taken.

(4) The interest in an eco-friendly and sustainable way of life is rising. People are using bikes, trains and buses instead of cars, recycling their rubbish, starting to buy more regional food, using less energy in their households and eating less meat.

Multiple Choice

Du musst eine inhaltlich passende Aussage zu einer Textpassage aus drei Antwortmöglichkeiten auswählen, die beim ersten Lesen alle einen gewissen Sinn ergeben. Hier ist immer nur eine Lösung richtig. Um einen Punkt zu erhalten, musst du außerdem einen Textbeleg in Form eines Kurzzitats liefern, sodass deutlich wird, dass du nicht geraten hast, sondern die richtige Textstelle gefunden hast. Eine reine Zeilenangabe genügt nicht. Bei diesen Belegen gibt es keinen Punktabzug für Rechtschreib- oder Grammatikfehler.

Beispielaufgabe und Musterlösung:

Many people …

a) ☐ have got used to the radical protests of some groups.

b) ☑ understand the motivation to demonstrate but do not like radical protest.

c) ☐ sympathise with very provocative forms of civil disobedience.

One piece of evidence from the text:

The majority [...] relate to their cause but do not approve of the measures

True/False

Du musst entscheiden, ob eine Aussage zu einer Textpassage richtig oder falsch ist. Denke auch hier immer an den Textbeleg in Form eines kurzen Zitats („One piece of evidence from the text“).

Beispielaufgabe und Musterlösung:

Many people understand the need to create awareness for global warming with the help of radical protest.

This statement is … ☐ true ☑ false

One piece of evidence from the text:

The majority [...] relate to their cause but do not approve of the measures

Filling in the Gaps/Short Answers

Du bist z. B. aufgefordert eine inhaltlich passende Kurzantwort in eine Aussage zum Text einzufügen oder einen Satzanfang einer Aussage zum Text sinnvoll zu vervollständigen.

Beispielaufgabe und Musterlösung:

Many people are aware of global warming and are changing their daily routine. However, most people do not agree with *forms of protest that are too radical*.

In ähnlicher Weise kann es sein, dass du eine inhaltlich passende Kurzantwort zu einer Frage zum Text formulieren oder Beispiele aus dem Text zu einem Thema anführen sollst. In der Musterlösung sind alle möglichen Antworten aufgelistet. Achte in der Prüfung aber genau auf Vorgaben wie „Name three things" und schreibe nicht weniger, aber auch nicht mehr.

Beispielaufgabe und Musterlösung:

Name three things people can do to reduce their carbon footprint in their everyday lives:

- *use public transport instead of cars / recycle rubbish*
- *buy more regional food / use less energy*
- *eat less meat*

Matching

Bei Zuordnungsaufgaben geht es in der Regel darum, die zentrale Aussage von Textabschnitten oder Kurztexten zu erfassen. Diese sollst du dann z. B. einer passenden Überschrift, einem Zitat oder einer Personenbeschreibung zuordnen. Oft gibt es auch ein oder mehrere Elemente, die zu keinem Abschnitt passen. Da es bei *Matching*-Aufgaben keine chronologisch angeordneten Teilaufgaben gibt, ist es hier besonders wichtig, dass du dir zunächst einen Überblick über den gesamten Text und alle Elemente verschaffst, die zugeordnet werden sollen.

Beispielaufgabe und Musterlösung:

Match the following quotes by citizens (A–E) with the correct text passages (1–4). There is one more quote than you need:

A "I have started buying vegetables, fruits and milk from the local farm shop."
B "The politicians should work harder to tackle the problem of global warming."
C "The problem is that other people may be affected and arrive too late for work."
D "It is a global challenge, but Europe could act as an international role model."
E "I totally understand the concerns but suggest different ways of voicing them."

Text passage	1	2	3	4
Quote	D	C	E	A

Strategien im Bereich Leseverstehen

Vorbereitung im Schullalltag

Auf diese Aufgaben kannst du dich grundsätzlich vorbereiten, indem du z. B.

- die Vokabeln deines Lehrbuchs und/oder anderer Materialien aus dem Unterricht regelmäßig wiederholst und so Inhalte schneller verstehst,
- regelmäßig englischsprachige (Online-)Artikel, Kommentare oder Jugendromane liest, die dich thematisch interessieren.

Tipps für die Bewältigung der Aufgaben

- Kläre zunächst für dich, **welche Art von Text** vorliegt (z. B. Romanauszug, Artikel).
- Brainstorme erste Gedanken zum **Thema** des Texts mithilfe der Überschrift und ggf. der Einleitung oder der enthaltenen Abbildungen. Je besser du dich auf das Thema einstellst, desto schneller kannst du den Text erfassen.
- Lies den Text nun in Ruhe zum ersten Mal durch und versuche zunächst, den Inhalt **allgemein** zu **verstehen**. Achte dabei darauf, ob ein Text in Abschnitte unterteilt ist. Teile ihn bei Bedarf in weitere Sinnabschnitte ein.
- Beim zweiten Lesen ist es hilfreich, am Rand kurze Überschriften oder die wichtigsten Schlüsselwörter zu den einzelnen Abschnitten zu notieren. So findest du dich beim Bearbeiten der Aufgaben schneller zurecht.
- Keine Sorge, wenn du nicht jedes Wort verstehst. Das ist nicht schlimm, denn vieles kannst du dir aus dem Zusammenhang erschließen.
- Lies dir dann die Aufgabenstellungen durch und markiere im Text die Stellen farbig, in denen du die nötigen Informationen findest. Notiere deine Antworten und vergiss auch die Textbelege nicht. Bei *Multiple Choice*, *True/False* und *Short Answers* kannst du der Reihe nach vorgehen, da die Teilaufgaben der Textchronologie folgen. Du kannst also davon ausgehen, dass du jeweils die Antwort zur nächsten Teilaufgabe im nächsten Textabschnitt findest.
- Falls du noch Zeit hast: Überprüfe am Ende deine Antworten noch einmal. Hast du alle Teilaufgaben beantwortet? Steht überall ein Textbeleg? Sind deine Antworten inhaltlich schlüssig?
- Die folgenden Übungen sind bewusst etwas herausfordernder gestaltet als es bisher in der ZP 10 üblich ist, sodass sie dich auch auf Aufgaben, z. B. in Klassenarbeiten an Gymnasien vorbereiten. Die Übungsaufgaben in Tests 1 bis 4 werden im Anspruch immer höher: Nr. 1 ist also deutlich leichter als Nr. 4.

Reading Test 1

(Neuseeland: kulturelle, soziale und politische Aspekte)

In dieser Übung trainierst du die Aufgabenformate, die auch in den Original-Prüfungen der letzten Jahre häufig vorkamen: eine Kombination aus Multiple Choice *und* True/False

Text

Bid[1] underway[2] in New Zealand to revive Māori language

by Phil Mercer

GISBORN, NEW ZEALAND – New Zealand has launched an official campaign to revive the indigenous Māori language. The ambitious project is part of an official strategy that sees the revival of the language as a key part in national identity and reconciliation.

The language has been surprisingly resilient[3] on its own. Case in point – an album by Māori heavy-metal band Alien Weaponry recently went straight to number one in New Zealand. But census data has shown that the number of indigenous speakers in the country has fallen.

Glenis Philip-Barbara, the former head of the Māori Language Commission, is optimistic about the future though.

"There aren't as many people speaking Māori as I'd like, I mean, around two-in-five Māori can have a conversation in te reo Māori (the Māori language), which is still quite low. But, look, we've made huge gains since the days when we were at two per cent. That was the 1970s, so we are steadily growing and, of course, without a proper command[4] of the language you don't actually have that in-depth understanding of your own culture," Philip-Barbara said.

Māori TV is publicly funded. Its presenters and journalists speak only in Māori.

It is a far cry[5] from when children were beaten or whipped at school for speaking their native tongue.

Tina Ngata, an indigenous rights campaigner, believes colonization has had terrible consequences for language.

"We talk about this idea of cultural genocide[6] and that one of the forms that colonization takes is that the policies, the legislation, the funding, the structures really lend itself towards only letting you survive if you survive as a colonial version of yourself, and it is much more difficult to survive as a Māori. Our resistance to that is to continue to flood our communities with beautiful Māori-speaking, Māori-singing ceremonial and contemporary versions and on-going, evolving versions of ourselves," Ngata said.

Millions of dollars of government money has been promised to help revitalize Māori. Like many other New Zealanders, the country's prime minister, Jacinta Ardern[7], is eager to learn.

"What is the most important thing in the world? The people, the people, the people," she said.

Words such as kia ora (hello), and kai (food) have long been part of New Zealand English. It is hoped that by 2040, one million Kiwis will be able to speak basic Māori.

Indigenous New Zealanders make up about 15% of the national population.

From: https://www.voanews.com/a/east-asia-pacific_bid-underway-new-zealand-revive-Māori-language/6178708.html

Annotations

1 **bid** – *hier: Antrag*
2 **to get sth underway** – *etwas ins Rollen bringen*
3 **resilient** – *widerstandsfähig*
4 **command** – *Beherrschung*
5 **it is a far cry from** – *das ist weit entfernt von*
6 **genocide** – *Völkermord*
7 **Jacinta Ardern** – NZ prime minister 2017–2023

Tasks

Tick (✓) the correct box **and give evidence** from the text.

HINT Read the text and the tasks carefully and highlight important passages.

1. The project can be regarded as part of the state's apology for mistakes made in its colonial past.

   This statement is … ☐ true ☐ false

   One piece of evidence from the text:

   ____

2. The Māori language is strong, as many people are fluent in it.

   This statement is … ☐ true ☐ false

   One piece of evidence from the text:

   ____

3. Glenis Philip-Barbara is …

   a) ☐ not sure about the survival of the indigenous language.

   b) ☐ content that more Māori speak the language than about 50 years ago.

   c) ☐ sad about the general lack of interest in the Māori language.

One piece of evidence from the text:

____

4. According to her, language is also key to indigenous heritage.
   This statement is … ☐ true ☐ false

   One piece of evidence from the text:

   ____

5. In the past, schoolchildren were subject to physical violence when they spoke Māori.
   This statement is … ☐ true ☐ false

   One piece of evidence from the text:

   ____

6. Tina Ngata believes that …
   a) ☐ there is not enough public funding to revive the language.
   b) ☐ her campaign for the survival of the culture is not supported enough by the state.
   c) ☐ the Māori were forced to adapt to the cultural concepts of their colonial masters.

   One piece of evidence from the text:

   ____

7. New Zealand's prime minister has been studying Māori intensively.
   This statement is … ☐ true ☐ false

   One piece of evidence from the text:

   ____

8. In the future more citizens will be offered the opportunity to become familiar with the indigenous language.
   This statement is … ☐ true ☐ false

   One piece of evidence from the text:

   ____

Lösungsvorschläge

1. The project can be regarded as part of the state's apology for mistakes made in its colonial past.

   This statement is … ☑ **true**

   Evidence: as a key part in […] reconciliation (ll. 3/4)

2. The Māori language is strong, as many people are fluent in it.

   This statement is … ☑ **false**

   Evidence: number of indigenous speakers in the country has fallen (ll. 7/8) / two-in-five Māori can have a conversation in te reo Māori […] low (ll. 11/12)

3. Glenis Philip-Barbara is …

   b) ☑ content that more Māori speak the language than about 50 years ago.

   Evidence: we've made huge gains (l. 13) / we are steadily growing (l. 14)

4. According to her, language is also key to indigenous heritage.

   This statement is … ☑ **true**

   Evidence: without […] command of the language you don't […] have that […] understanding of your own culture (ll. 15/16)

5. In the past, schoolchildren were subject to physical violence when they spoke Māori. This statement is … ☑ **true**

   Evidence: when children were beaten or whipped at school for speaking their native tongue (ll. 18/19)

6. Tina Ngata believes that …

   c) ☑ the Māori were forced to adapt to the cultural concepts of their colonial masters.

   Evidence: (one of the forms that colonization takes […]) only letting you survive if you survive as a colonial version of yourself (ll. 22–25)

7. New Zealand's prime minister has been studying Māori intensively.

   This statement is … ☑ **false**

   Evidence: the country's prime minister […] is eager to learn (ll. 30/31)

8. In the future more citizens will be offered the opportunity to become familiar with the indigenous language.

   This statement is … ☑ **true**

   Evidence: by 2040, one million Kiwis will be able to speak basic Māori (ll. 35/36)

Reading Test 2

(Alltag und Freizeitgestaltung, Konsum und Verbraucherschutz)

■ *In dieser Übung trainierst du das* True/False-*Format.*

Text **Giving teenagers alcohol may increase risk of drink-related problems** by Nicola Davis

Parents offering even limited amounts of alcohol may increase risk of binge-drinking and other problems, study concludes

Parents who give alcohol to their teenagers could be increasing[1] their children's risk of binge drinking[2] and other alcohol-related problems, research has revealed.

The study found that compared with secondary-school aged children who had no access to alcohol, those who were given some by their parents more often admitted to later binge drinking, had symptoms of alcohol-use disorder and experienced alcohol-related damage – such as difficulty recalling events or getting into trouble.

The authors conclude there is no evidence that parental supply of alcohol protects children from such experiences.

"It is, unfortunately, well-intentioned[3], but not a good idea," said Richard Mattick, professor of drug and alcohol studies at the University of New South Wales and a co-author of the research. "All you are doing is giving your permission to kids to drink."

Writing in *The Lancet Public Health*, Mattick and colleagues describe how they followed the behaviours of more than 1,900 parents and secondary-school aged children over the course of six years, from around the age of 12 until they reached sixth form[4].

Perhaps unsurprisingly, the team found that experience of alcohol-related damage and binge drinking – where five or more drinks are consumed in one sitting – increased as the children grew older.

But while previous[5] research from the team had suggested parental supply of alcohol did not increase risk of children binge-drinking, and resulted in a lower risk of drinking overall compared with those who obtained it from elsewhere, such as friends, the new study suggests that parental supply does not protect children from consuming alcohol excessively.

Taking into account factors including children's sex, age, and household income, children who had been given alcohol by parents alone had 2.58 times the odds[6] of reporting binge-drinking in the following year, compared with those with no supply of alcohol; the odds of alcohol-related harm or symptoms of alcohol use disorder were also more than twice as high as for those with no supply.

The odds were even higher for the children who got hold of alcohol from other sources, either in addition to or instead of parental supply, with these children also found to have higher chances of alcohol abuse or dependency symptoms than those who had no alcohol supply – although such questions were only asked of older teens. While 25% of teens around 18 years old who were given alcohol by their parents reported binge-drinking, the figure reached 62% for those obtaining alcohol from elsewhere and 81% for those receiving alcohol from parents and others.

While the impact of the quantity[7] of alcohol supplied by parents is yet to be published, the latest study reveals that even sips of alcohol given by parents double the odds of children receiving alcohol from other sources in the following year, with the impact even greater if parents supplied whole drinks.

The authors admit that the research has limitations, including that it relied on self-report […]. But they say its size, and the fact it looked at children into their late teens, meant it was better able to analyse the impact of parental alcohol supply than the previous report.

Mattick adds that the team has recently received funding to follow the teenagers to the age of 23. "The story isn't fully told until we can determine whether this leads to the real harm, which is alcohol use disorders," he said.

From: Nicola Davis: Giving teenagers alcohol may increase risk of drink-related problems – study, https://www.theguardian.com/society/2018/jan/25/giving-teenagers-alcohol-may-increase-risk-of-drink-related-problems-study (slightly adapted), Copyright Guardian

Annotations

1 **to increase** – *erhöhen*
2 **binge drinking** – excessive consumption of alcohol
3 **intention** – *Absicht*
4 **sixth form** – *Abschlussklasse, z. B. in England (vergleichbar mit der Oberstufe in Deutschland)*
5 **previous** – preceding, former, earlier
6 **odds** – chances
7 **quantity** – *Quantität, Menge, Ausmaß*

Tasks

Decide whether the following information is **true or false** and tick (✓) the correct box. Give one piece of **evidence** from the text.

1. The new study shows that children who do not drink any alcohol experience more alcohol-related problems later in life.

   This statement is … ☐ true ☐ false

   One piece of evidence from the text:

   ___

2. Some parents mean well when they sometimes allow their children to drink alcohol.

   This statement is … ☐ true ☐ false

   One piece of evidence from the text:

   ___

3. About one thousand parents participated in the study.

   This statement is … ☐ true ☐ false

   One piece of evidence from the text:

   ___

4. The experts did not find younger children who had as much as five alcoholic drinks in one period.

   This statement is … ☐ true ☐ false

   One piece of evidence from the text:

   ___

5. Studies from the past showed that children were more protected from alcohol-related problems when they had drunk alcohol in the presence of their parents and not somewhere else.

   This statement is … ☐ true ☐ false

   One piece of evidence from the text:

   ___

6. The new study also focused on the parental economic background.
   This statement is … ☐ true ☐ false
   One piece of evidence from the text:
   ____

7. According to the study, the risk of binge drinking among young adults more than doubles when they are given alcohol outside their household.
   This statement is … ☐ true ☐ false
   One piece of evidence from the text:
   ____

8. As a parent it is wiser to allow your children to try a whole alcoholic drink rather than only let them taste it.
   This statement is … ☐ true ☐ false
   One piece of evidence from the text:
   ____

9. The recent study meets all professional and academic standards.
   This statement is … ☐ true ☐ false
   One piece of evidence from the text:
   ____

10. The next study project will focus on young adults.
    This statement is … ☐ true ☐ false
    One piece of evidence from the text:
    ____

HINT

In der Musterlösung geben wir dir als Hilfe unter „Evidence" auch die Zeilen des Texts in Klammern an, in denen du ein passendes Zitat findest. In der Prüfung brauchst du keine Zeilenverweise anzugeben. Vorsicht, wenn du nur die Zeilenangabe als Antwort aufschreibst, bekommst du keinen Punkt.

1. The new study shows that children who do not drink any alcohol experience more alcohol-related problems later in life.

   This statement is … ☑ **false**

   Evidence: Parents offering even limited amounts of alcohol may increase risk of binge-drinking and other problems (cf. introduction) / The study found that […] those who were given some [alcohol] by their parents more often admitted to later binge drinking (ll. 3–5)

2. Some parents mean well when they sometimes allow their children to drink alcohol.

   This statement is … ☑ **true**

   Evidence: parental supply of alcohol […] is […] well-intentioned, but not a good idea (ll. 9/10)

3. About one thousand parents participated in the study.

   This statement is … ☑ **false**

   Evidence: they followed the behaviours of more than 1,900 parents and secondary-school aged children (ll. 14–16)

4. The experts did not find younger children who had as much as five alcoholic drinks in one period.

   This statement is … ☑ **false**

   Evidence: binge drinking – where five or more drinks are consumed in one sitting – increased as the children grew older (ll. 19/20)

5. Studies from the past showed that children were more protected from alcohol-related problems when they had drunk alcohol in the presence of their parents and not somewhere else.

   This statement is … ☑ **true**

   Evidence: previous research […] had suggested parental supply of alcohol did not increase risk of children binge-drinking (ll. 21/22)

6. The new study also focused on the parental economic background.
   This statement is … ☑ **true**
   Evidence: Taking into account factors including […] household income (ll. 26/27)
7. According to the study, the risk of binge drinking among young adults more than doubles when they are given alcohol outside their household.
   This statement is … ☑ **true**
   Evidence: While 25% of teens around 18 years old who were given alcohol by their parents reported binge-drinking, the figure reached 62% (ll. 35/36)
8. As a parent it is wiser to allow your children to try a whole alcoholic drink rather than only let them taste it.
   This statement is … ☑ **false**
   Evidence: even sips of alcohol given by parents double the odds of children […] with the impact even greater if parents supplied whole drinks. (ll. 39–41)
9. The recent study meets all professional and academic standards.
   This statement is … ☑ **false**
   Evidence: The authors admit that the research has limitations, including that it relied on self-report (ll. 42/43)
10. The next study project will focus on young adults.
    This statement is … ☑ **true**
    Evidence: the team has recently received funding to follow the teenagers to the age of 23 (ll. 46/47)

Reading Test 3

(Lebensstile in der peer group, *Demokratie und Menschenrechte)*

■ *Hier trainierst du* Multiple-Choice-, True/False- *und* Short Answers-*Aufgaben.*

Text

At last, a generation of schoolchildren will grow up knowing it's OK to be LGBT[1] by Paul Twocock

Next year, all primary schools must teach pupils that different types of families exist. It is a great step forward for society

Students across the country are heading back to school this week, and while this might not seem momentous, for Stonewall[2], this school year marks the beginning of the end of a decades-long campaign to get an inclusive education system in England.[3] […] It will be a historic moment – a whole generation will attend schools that not only accept LGBT people and same-sex relationships, but also celebrate and offer support on the issues that young LGBT people face.

The guidance means that primary schools will teach about different families, which of course includes LGBT families. Contrary to what's been said by some online and in the media, this is just about showing kids that families can have two mums or two dads. Or to put another way: different families, same love.

If you, like me, were at school in the 1980s and 90s you endured an education system that erased LGBT people and history. In 1989, section 28[4] banned local authorities from "promoting homosexuality". Without any recognition or inclusion, and with teachers essentially banned from harshly criticising those who used homophobic insults, bullying flourished and badly traumatised a generation of young people. Growing up as a gay boy in Kent[5] was hard. Schools couldn't even acknowledge the existence of gay people, let alone talk about the challenges we faced – I felt totally isolated and afraid of being found out. All the while, the media wrote stories about lesbian, gay and bi people arguing that children would be "turned" gay if they were taught about same-sex relationships. I had few role models and was left feeling ashamed of who I was. During my entire school career I couldn't accept my sexuality, let alone be open about it.

The struggle to remove section 28 took years. It only left the statute books[6] in 2000 in Scotland and 2003 in England and Wales. Kent county council even voted to keep its own version of section 28, and that was only stopped when the 2010 Equality Act[7] came into force. […] Teaching about LGBT families not only means children from these families see themselves reflected in what they learn, but also helps all young people understand that there's nothing wrong or unusual about being LGBT.

However, if this is to be effective, the government (whoever that might be) has to invest in training to prepare teachers and schools. All schools need to have the resources and time to engage with parents and carers, and explain how they will teach these subjects in a way that benefits children from all backgrounds. To make this happen, we want people to write to their local authorities and be vocal in their support for inclusive education, so that every child can grow up and reach their full potential.

We know that 60% of the British public want primary school teachers to talk positively about different kinds of families, including those who are LGBT, to their students. We work in many schools where young people are already embedding LGBT inclusion in their schools – because it's so important for them. […]

Inclusive teaching is an affirmation that you exist, and your identity is valid. It's also not just about lesbian, gay, bi and trans people. It's crucial that people realise that there's no hierarchy in this teaching. It's about acceptance for people from all backgrounds – be that race, gender, sexual orientation, faith, class and/or disability. This kind of teaching will help foster greater inclusion, acceptance and understanding in our classrooms, playgrounds and school corridors.

I'm under no illusion that it will be plain sailing[8] or that there'll be no more disruptions outside schools. A vocal minority have gained a platform with anti-diversity rhetoric that seeks to target LGBT people and divide communities. Some protesters claim that a move towards inclusive education is against their religion. This supports a harmful myth that faith and LGBT inclusion cannot coexist. […]

Inclusive education helps to create inclusive communities. Building a more welcoming society requires building bridges between diverse groups. If all schools teach acceptance – no exceptions – then that would be a good first step to healing some of the division that we've seen in society over the past decade.

From: Paul Twocock: At last, a generation of schoolchildren will grow up knowing it's OK to be LGBT, https://www.theguardian.com/commentisfree/2019/sep/05/schools-teach-lgbt-september-2020-new-regulations (slightly adapted), Copyright Guardian News & Media Ltd 2023

Annotations

1 **LGBT** – **l**esbian, **g**ay, **b**isexual, **t**ransgender
2 **Stonewall** – influential LGBT rights charity organisation in the UK
3 In September 2020, new regulations for teaching relationships and sex education (RSE) in English schools came into force.
4 **section 28** – law from 1988 that forbids the "promotion of homosexuality" by local authorities
5 **Kent** – county in England
6 **statute book** – *Gesetzbuch*
7 **Equality Act** – anti-discrimination law
8 **plain sailing** – without any problems

Tasks

Tick (✓) the correct box **and give evidence** from the text or give short answers.

1. The author Paul Twocock is happy because …
   - a) ☐ students are organising campaigns to make the education system in England inclusive.
   - b) ☐ with the new law on teaching relationships and sex education LGBT students will also get advice in class.
   - c) ☐ the media supports primary schools teaching students about different families.

   One piece of evidence from the text:

   ____

2. In the 1980s and '90s …
   - a) ☐ teachers could not actually stop the bullying of gay students.
   - b) ☐ some teachers didn't want to tell homophobic bullies to stop.
   - c) ☐ people criticised the existence of gay people at schools.

   One piece of evidence from the text:

   ____

3. When the author went to school, some people feared that students would become gay if they learned about same-sex relationships.

   This statement is … ☐ true ☐ false

   One piece of evidence from the text:

   ____

4. When Paul Twocock wanted to come out at school, there were only a few role models to help him.

   This statement is … ☐ true ☐ false

   One piece of evidence from the text:

   ____

5. The author's hometown got rid of section 28 in 2003.

   This statement is … ☐ true ☐ false

   One piece of evidence from the text:

   ____

6. What helps to improve inclusive education and teaching? Name three examples.
   - ______________________________
   - ______________________________
   - ______________________________

7. Inclusive education …
   a) ☐ provokes more conflict among students and parents.
   b) ☐ stops bullying and discrimination in primary schools.
   c) ☐ shows gay students that their way of life is accepted in society.

   One piece of evidence from the text:

   ____

8. The author personally holds the view that …
   a) ☐ inclusive education is against the religious beliefs of some protesters.
   b) ☐ LGBT inclusion and religion cannot coexist.
   c) ☐ a few people will protest loudly with discriminating slogans against inclusive education.

   One piece of evidence from the text:

   ____

9. Finish the following sentence in your own words:

   The author believes that inclusive communities are good for society because

   ____

Lösungsvorschläge

HINT

In Klammern sind als Hilfe wieder die Textstellen angegeben, in denen du die möglichen Belege („evidence") findest.

1. The author Paul Twocock is happy because …

   b) ☑ with the new law on teaching relationships and sex education LGBT students will also get advice in class.

   Evidence: It is a great step forward for society (intro) / new regulations for teaching […] came into force (Annotation 3) / attend schools that […] offer support on the issues that young LGBT people face (ll. 4–6)

2. In the 1980s and '90s …

   a) ☑ teachers could not actually stop the bullying of gay students.

   Evidence: with teachers essentially banned from harshly criticising those who used homophobic insults (ll. 14/15) / Schools couldn't even acknowledge the existence of gay people (ll. 16/17)

3. When the author went to school, some people feared that students would become gay if they learned about same-sex relationships.

   This statement is … ☑ **true**

   Evidence: the media […] arguing that children would be "turned" gay if they were taught about same-sex relationships (ll. 18–20)

4. When Paul Twocock wanted to come out at school, there were only a few role models to help him.

   This statement is … ☑ **false**

   Evidence: During my entire school career I couldn't accept my sexuality, let alone be open about it (ll. 21/22)

5. The author's hometown got rid of section 28 in 2003.

   This statement is … ☑ **false**

   Evidence: Kent County Council even voted to keep its own version of section 28 (ll. 24/25)

6. *mögliche Lösungen:*
   - invest in training to prepare teachers and schools
   - provide schools with resources for programmes

- explain the subject matter to parents and carers
- write to local authorities and ask for support

7. Inclusive education …

   c) ☑ shows gay students that their way of life is accepted in society.

   Evidence: is an affirmation that you exist, and your identity is valid (l. 41) / It's about acceptance for people from all backgrounds (ll. 43/44)

8. The author personally holds the view that …

   c) ☑ a few people will protest loudly with discriminating slogans against inclusive education.

   Evidence: A vocal minority have gained a platform with anti-diversity rhetoric that seeks to target LGBT people (ll. 48/49)

9. The author believes that inclusive communities are good for society because **they are welcoming. /**
   they create bridges between different people/different groups of people. /
   they help to heal divisions in society.

Reading Test 4

(Berufsprofile im digitalen Zeitalter, wirtschaftlich-technologische Aspekte)

■ *In dieser Übung trainierst du das Aufgabenformat* Matching.

Text **Jobs of the future: are you ready to join in?** by Zofia Niemtus

If you want to reskill[1], a tech-related postgraduate[2] course could future-proof your career

(1) We are in the middle of a fourth industrial revolution. The first saw the world move from rural societies to industrial urban centres; the second introduced mass production; and the third brought the digital revolution. The fourth is changing how we integrate technology into our lives, thanks to advances such as artificial intelligence (AI), nanotechnology and robotics. But what will this mean for humans as workers?

(2) Retraining will be an essential feature of the new employment landscape, in which many jobs will be automated. Opportunities to reskill should be offered across the whole economy and supported by tax relief to ensure the UK is prepared for the changes ahead, a recent Social Market Foundation report suggested.

(3) Postgraduate study is already a popular option for those looking to move their career in a new direction. Jean-Marc Frangos, a managing director based in Silicon Valley at BT, one of the UK's largest technology employers, has observed that a growing number of people working in tech retrained after studying for unrelated first degrees.

"When I meet people here, their original education might be anything from ancient Greek to marketing," he says. "Now they work in the tech domain and they're very good. Don't assume that your original education is excluding you from a tech career."

(4) There are a wide variety of tech careers available for people to pursue after further study, he continues, but certain areas will be in greater demand – particularly data science analytics and cybersecurity, both of which are offered at master's level at universities across the country. A recent report from jobs site *Indeed* named data scientists and cybersecurity experts among the most "future-proof" careers.

(5) AI, too, is a huge growth industry: a report from jobs site *Indeed* found that employer demand for AI-related roles has more than doubled in the US in the past three years, while the number of jobseekers looking for those roles has remained roughly the same. In 2017, the UK government recommended creating an industry-funded AI master's programme.

Caroline Jay is a senior lecturer in the school of computer science at the University of Manchester and teaches on the "AI: Robot overlord, replacement or colleague?" module. The course is available to students from all disciplines, she explains, and teaches the theory underpinning[3] AI, as well as practical experience of programming.

(6) "We're seeing more students from the sciences and social sciences, and even some from humanities," she says. "They're not trained in computer science as a first degree, but they do start to do bits of programming and coding along the way and realise it gives them a huge advantage over people who can't."

Even if students don't end up working in AI, she says, the skills they develop on the course will be invaluable in an increasingly tech-driven jobs market.

(7) "We've changed the way we think about technology," she says. "If you have people who are experts in accounting or law or medicine or fashion design and they understand how technology could help them with that, they can be the ones to drive it forward. They might not be writing the programmes, but they will be leading the problem-solving aspect of it. They can make those informed decisions that people in the professions are going to need in the future."

(8) Nicola Webb is studying for an MSc in data science and computational intelligence at Coventry University, and is hoping to go on to research social robotics – which looks at advances such as using robots to take care of the elderly. She says the potential for development in this area is vast.

"We often debate whether we should be developing AI to such an intelligent level," she says. "But I think that this generation of computer and data scientists are more than aware of the dangers, through their own research, or from sci-fi movies like *Ex Machina*, that put such scenarios into play. There is so much that AI can do for us in the future, and we shouldn't be scared to develop it."

(9) She recommends anyone considering postgraduate study in the field to "brush up on mathematics, especially linear algebra and matrices", as there is "much more maths involved than you think".

Frangos agrees, stating that "excellent technical credentials" will always be necessary, but that the right mindset[4] is by far the most valuable skill to develop.

"Have a proactive attitude," he says. "It might look complicated because it looks scientific, but there's a lot of democratisation taking place. There's a lot of fluidity[5] in this new tech world. It's not an exclusive world, and it's particularly welcoming to people who have curious and open minds."

From: Zofia Niemtus: Jobs of the future: are you ready to join in?, https://www.theguardian.com/education/2019/jan/22/jobs-of-the-future-are-you-ready-to-join-in (slightly adapted), Copyright Guardian News & Media Ltd 2023

Annotations

1 **to reskill** – to train or study sth. different
2 **postgraduate (course/study)** – *Aufbaustudium*
3 **underpinning** – here: which is the basis of
4 **mindset** – attitude
5 **fluidity** – flexibility

Task

The following headings (A–J) sum up the main information in each paragraph of the article. Choose the best heading for each text passage (1–9). There is one more heading than you need.

A Broad-mindedness – a key qualification for a tech career

B Increasing job demands linked to AI may lead to new university courses sponsored by companies

C Useful input for professionals to improve tech processes in their fields of work

D The eras of economic and technological development

E Automation of jobs will cause unemployment in certain fields of work

F 'Artificial Intelligence' programmes as follow-up studies – always helpful for any graduate

G The necessity of government support to develop new competencies

H Benefits and ethical concerns surrounding Artificial Intelligence

I More and more academics from different domains succeeding in a tech-driven field of work

J A prospering job market: the analysis and protection of information

Paragraph	1	2	3	4	5	6	7	8	9
Heading									

HINT **Blindtext**

Einzelne Überschriften scheinen auf den ersten Blick vielleicht zu mehreren Textstellen zu passen. Im Folgenden kannst du nachvollziehen, warum eine Überschrift in besonderer Weise auf ihre jeweilige Passage zutrifft:

1–D: Hier werden die vier Zeitalter im Kontext einer „industrial revolution“ (Z. 1) skizziert.

2–G: Zu Abschnitt 2 könnte man auch an E denken, da die Stichwörter „job“ und „automated“ vorkommen. Die Hauptaussage ist aber die Forderung nach Weiterbildung, gefördert durch die Regierung, was sich widerspiegelt in: „supported by tax relief to ensure the UK is prepared for the changes ahead“ (Z. 9/10).

3–I: I scheint zunächst auch kombinierbar mit 6, die Betonung „more and more academics“ weist aber auf Abschnitt 3 als passendere Wahl: a “**growing number** of people working in tech retrained after studying for unrelated first degrees” (Z. 13–15)

4–J: „particularly data science analytics and cybersecurity“ (Z. 21/22), „named data scientists and cybersecurity experts among the most ‘future-proof’ careers“ (Z. 24/25)

5–B: “the UK government recommended creating an industry-funded AI master’s programme” (Z. 29/30)

6–F: Hier mögen auf den ersten Blick auch C oder I infrage kommen, treffender ist aber F: “Even if students don’t end up working in AI, [...] the skills they develop on the course will be invaluable in an increasingly tech-driven jobs market.” (Z. 40/41)

7–C: “They might not be writing the programmes, but they will be leading the problem-solving aspect of it.” (Z. 45/46)

8–H: vgl. Z. 53–56

9–A: Der Begriff „broad-mindedness“ (A) findet sich wieder in Aussagen wie „the right mindset“ (Z. 61), „a proactive attitude“ (Z. 62) und „people who have curious and open minds“ (Z. 65).

Überschrift E passt zu keinem der Abschnitte.

Paragraph	1	2	3	4	5	6	7	8	9
Heading	D	G	I	J	B	F	C	H	A

Wortschatz

Im Prüfungsteil Wortschatz wird dir ein Text vorgelegt, in den verschiedene Arten von Aufgaben „eingebaut“ sind. Die möglichen Aufgabenformen werden dir in diesem Kapitel vorgestellt. Normalerweise behandeln Wortschatzaufgabe und Schreibaufgabe der ZP 10 dasselbe Thema, sodass du dich mit dem Wortschatzteil schon auf das Thema der nachfolgenden Aufgaben einstimmen kannst.

Gute Wortschatzkenntnisse helfen dir aber natürlich nicht nur in diesem Prüfungsteil, sondern sind auch für alle anderen Kompetenzbereiche sehr wichtig.

Allgemeine Hinweise

Das Ergebnis macht 10 % des Endergebnisses aus. Du bekommst Punkte für richtige Inhalte und insgesamt max. 4 Zusatzpunkte für die korrekte Rechtschreibung und richtige grammatikalische Verwendung von Begriffen, die du in Lückentexte einsetzt: Du erkennst zum Beispiel richtig, dass ein Nomen im Plural oder ein Verb in der *-ing*-Form eingefügt werden muss.

Beispiel für eine Punktevergabe:
20 Punkte „Inhalt“ + 4 Zusatzpunkte „korrekte Sprache“ = **24 Punkte**

Im Prüfungsteil Wortschatz zeigst du, dass du Bedeutungen im Zusammenhang erschließen und wiedererkennen kannst und den Wortschatz spezifischer Themenfelder auch aktiv anwenden kannst.

Häufige Aufgabenformate

Multiple Choice

Für eine Lücke im Text musst du eine inhaltlich passende Wendung aus vier Antwortmöglichkeiten auswählen. Hier gibt es immer nur **eine richtige Lösung** (jeweils ein Punkt pro Teilaufgabe).

Beispiel:

More and more people are affected by the climate crisis and ...

a) ☐ are getting used to ... b) ☐ are taking advantage of ...

c) ☐ are responsible for ... d) ☑ are becoming aware of ...

the benefits of a more sustainable lifestyle.

Tipp: Im ersten Moment scheinen ggf. mehrere Antwortmöglichkeiten sinnvoll. Logisch und 100 % passend ist aber nur Antwort d).

Filling in the Gaps

Du bist aufgefordert ein inhaltlich passendes Wort in eine Lücke einzufügen. Hier gibt es oft mehrere mögliche Lösungen (jeweils zwei Punkte pro Lücke).

Beispiel:

More and more people are affected by the climate crisis and are becoming aware of the benefits / idea / advantages / necessity of a more sustainable lifestyle.

Tipp: Hier gibt es meistens mindestens drei sehr gut passende Antwortoptionen und weitere, die ebenfalls in Ordnung sind.

Matching

Es könnte auch sein, dass du z. B. die Bedeutung bestimmter englischsprachiger Begriffe kennen und diese einer Aussage oder einem Synonym richtig zuordnen sollst. (Beispiel: siehe Test 1, Task 3)

Mind-mapping

Ein weiterer möglicher Aufgabentyp ist, dass du eine themengebundene Mindmap mit einer bestimmten Anzahl von Begriffen erstellst. (Beispiel: siehe Training 2, Task 1)

Wichtiger Hinweis: In den letzten Prüfungen gab es immer eine Kombination von *Multiple Choice* und *Filling in the Gaps*. Aus diesem Grund sind auch die nachfolgenden Übungen überwiegend mit diesen Aufgabentypen gestaltet.

Strategien im Bereich Wortschatz

Vorbereitung im Schulalltag

Auf diese Aufgaben kannst du dich grundsätzlich vorbereiten, indem du z. B.

- die Vokabeln deines Lehrbuchs und/oder anderer Materialien aus dem Unterricht regelmäßig lernst und in längeren Zeitabständen wiederholst (→ Vokabelheft, Mindmaps, Karteikarten, Apps usw.).
- viele dieser neuen Wörter, Begriffe und Redewendungen bewusst in Texten verwendest, die du selber in Übungen im Unterricht und zu Hause schreibst.
- regelmäßig englischsprachige (Online-)Artikel, Kommentare oder Jugendromane liest bzw. Filme und Serien ansiehst, Podcasts anhörst etc., die dich thematisch interessieren.

Praktische Tipps zum Vokabellernen vor Prüfungen

Finde für dich heraus, wie du am besten und am liebsten Vokabeln visualisierst und lernst. Strukturiere z. B. die Vokabeln nach Themenfeldern und fertige eine Liste, Tabelle oder Mindmap an. Arbeite mit unterschiedlichen Farben und Symbolen und mache dir ein Foto davon mit dem Smartphone, das du immer parat hast. Am besten bleiben Vokabeln im Kopf, wenn du aktiv damit arbeitest.
Gestalte ein Themenset von kleinen Karteikarten (Vorderseite: englischer Begriff, Rückseite: dt. Begriff oder Bild, Symbol, Synonym, andere Wortart etc.). Packe das aktuelle Kartenset in deine Tasche, Jacke o. Ä., sodass du spontan (z. B. in der U-Bahn, im Bus) die Begriffe wiederholen kannst.

Weitere Tipps und Strategien zum Vokabellernen kannst du dir in diesem Video ansehen. Scanne dazu einfach den nebenstehenden Code.

Vocabulary Training 1: Growing up

(Alltag und Freizeitgestaltung, Identitätssuche)

Task 1

Complete the following **table** with a word from the same word family. You may use an online dictionary.

German (for the noun)	Noun	Verb (phrase)	Adjective
		to reach puberty	pubescent
Kritik			critical
Errungenschaft		to achieve sth	---
Rebellion	rebellion		
		to attract sb	
Sozialisation		to socialize	
		to form an opinion	
	experience	to (gain) experience	
(Un-)Angepasstheit		to (not) conform to	
		to challenge sb	

Task 2

Use a suitable English expression from the table above to **fill in** the text about growing up.

Grown-ups often **(1)** ____________________ adolescents because they think they are not mature enough or too **(2)** ______________________. Moreover, parents don't want their kids to only hang around with people from their peer group. For parents as well as teenagers **(3)** ______________________ can be a difficult period in life. Young people sometimes **(4)** ____________________ against the rules at home and there are many differences of **(5)** ____________________.
Life can be a **(6)** ______________________ for teenagers when they are searching for their identity. They experiment, **(7)** _________________________ to boys or girls and have new experiences. Many of them want to **(8)** ____________________ something in life. They often identify with role models they look up to.

Lösungsvorschläge

Task 1

German (for the noun)	**Noun**	**Verb (phrase)**	**Adjective**
Pubertät	**puberty**	to reach puberty	pubescent
Kritik	**criticism**	**to criticise sb/sth**	critical
Errungenschaft	**achievement**	to achieve sth	---
Rebellion	rebellion	**to rebel**	**rebellious**
Anziehung, Anziehungskraft	**attraction**	to attract sb	**attractive**
Sozialisation	**socialisation**	to socialise	**social**
Meinung	**opinion**	to form an opinion	**opinionated** *(abwertend)*
Erfahrung	experience	to (gain) experience	**experienced**
(Un-)Angepasstheit	**(non-)conformity**	to (not) conform to	**(non-)conformist**
Herausforderung	**challenge**	to challenge sb	**challenging**

Task 2

(1) criticise
(2) (non-)conformist/ rebellious/opinionated
(3) puberty
(4) rebel
(5) opinion
(6) challenge
(7) feel attraction/ are attracted
(8) achieve/ experience

Vocabulary Training 2: Safe sex & teenage pregnancy

(Jugendkulturen: Verantwortung, Liebe & Freundschaft)

Task 1

Study the following expressions and arrange them in a **mind map** on a separate sheet of paper. Make sure you are familiar with their meaning. You can write a (German) translation next to words you don't know in a different colour.

helpline • sexual intercourse • to be on the pill • STD (sexually transmitted disease) • abortion • counselling (e. g. on pregnancy options) • (sexual) maturity • to practise safe sex • fertile • contraceptive • pregnancy test • promiscuity • birth control • to date sb • to be jealous of sb • to make love to sb • sexual orientation • to date sb • to be in a relationship • to exert pressure on sb • role model

Task 2

Choose the right place for some of these words in the following text on teenage pregnancy:

When young people fall in love, they sometimes decide to have **(1)** ______________________________ in their relationship. Parents and teachers tell them that they should always **(2)** ______________________: Young couples are often advised to use **(3)** __________________ to avoid an unwanted pregnancy, for example. Being on **(4)** ______________________ can be one option for girls. Condoms are also an alternative. Everyone should be aware that not all of these options can prevent **(5)** __________________. Pregnant teenage girls or boys who are about to become young fathers often do not feel mature enough for parenthood and may get help by getting **(6)** __________________. You can call a **(7)** __________________, for example. Professionals will guide you to find medical support from a doctor nearby and may also inform you of your options, such as the benefits and challenges of young parenthood, the possibility of adoption or the rules on **(8)** __________________. You can also always seek help from experienced people you trust, like a social worker or a teacher at your school.

Lösungsvorschläge

Task 1

individual solutions

Task 2

(1) sex(ual intercourse)
(2) practise safe sex
(3) contraceptives
(4) the pill
(5) STDs / sexually transmitted diseases
(6) counselling
(7) helpline
(8) abortion

Vocabulary Test 1: Digital life & communication

(Berufsprofile im digitalen Zeitalter in Auckland)

In dieser Übung trainierst du die Aufgabenformate Multiple Choice, Filling in the Gaps *und* Matching *in separaten Teilaufgaben.*

HINT First, read the whole interview with a digital world designer from Auckland (New Zealand). Try to get the gist of the text before you start doing the tasks. That makes it much easier to do the tasks afterwards.

Task 1

Choose the expression that fits the context best.

1. **Journalist:** Dr Chang. Thank you very much for offering the …

   a) ☐ opportunity b) ☐ moment c) ☐ pleasure d) ☐ option

   to talk to you about communication in the past and present, life in Auckland – the "tech powerhouse" of New Zealand – and your work as a digital world designer.

2. And here comes my first question: have you always been fascinated by technological …

   a) ☐ movement? b) ☐ progress?
   c) ☐ interventions? d) ☐ productivity?

3. **Dr Chang:** Thank you for having me. Well, the technology in my childhood was not as advanced or complex as it is nowadays, of course. In the 1980s, people mostly wrote letters and made phone calls. In the '90s, people started …

   a) ☐ postponing b) ☐ distributing
   c) ☐ collecting d) ☐ furthering

   information very easily on the internet.

4. A lot of data could be …

   a) ☐ shifted b) ☐ pushed c) ☐ wired d) ☐ transferred

   from one place to another with the help of wireless communication.

5. Since the beginning of the new millennium, all sorts of social networks have been emerging and connect people from all over the world. Now, there is a new focus …

   a) ☐ on b) ☐ in c) ☐ of d) ☐ to

   artificial intelligence and all kinds of virtual realities.

   Journalist: And in New Zealand, Auckland is considered one of the centres of inspiration in the tech domain.

6. **Dr Chang:** Absolutely. Influential companies have discovered the region and its perfect infrastructure, and their campuses are starting to …

   a) ☐ catch b) ☐ grab c) ☐ attract d) ☐ combine

   graduates who feel an affinity for technology as well as digitalism and show a profound curiosity about future trends.

7. You get in touch …

   a) ☐ by b) ☐ via c) ☐ since d) ☐ with

   creative people from all walks of life and different ethnic backgrounds.

8. The atmosphere in that area is full of energy and positivity …

   a) ☐ as b) ☐ due to c) ☐ because d) ☐ for

   the rich cultural and diverse spirit of its population.

Task 2

Fill in suitable words or expressions so that the text makes sense.
Try on your own first, but if you need help: Take a look at the **vocab box** below the text passage.

1. **Journalist:** Young graduates in particular are said to face new difficulties on the job market, the automation of work routines being one of them. In your opinion, what ________________ do job descriptions require nowadays?

2. **Dr Chang:** First of all, I must beg to differ – I take a different ________________ here, as there are new kinds of jobs for academics and other professions that are constantly being created.

3. But to answer your question: if you intend to ________________ in the tech industry, flexibility, adaptability, enthusiasm and teamwork will be crucial for your employability. The way in which we view work has changed.

4. Today, you can ________________ a variety of work options over the course of your professional career, which is great.
5. I must admit though that it *does* look like there will be a need in the future to keep on acquiring new competencies and there will probably be more ________ ____________ in the world of work. So people will simply have to adapt accordingly.
6. A healthy work-life balance could help you to develop some sort of ________ ____________.

Help

resilience • explore/gain experience in • qualifications • skills • view/perspective • pursue/follow a career • competition

Task 3

Match a synonym (or an expression very close to the meaning of the original word) to each of the words underlined (1 to 11) by putting in the correct number in the table below. There is an example (0) at the beginning.

to analyse	Besides	scenery	course	to create	creative ideas

	0				
fascinated	dealing	example	to make easier	material	traits

Journalist: What is your personal strategy for **(0)** coping with stress and pressure in your profession?

Dr Chang: I try to separate my private life from my work life. For **(1)** instance, I do not talk about business when I meet my friends. I enjoy the rich nature of New Zealand on weekend trips or simple activities like swimming, hiking or running before or after work. **(2)** Moreover, the wilderness sometimes gives me **(3)** inspiration for my digital projects.

Journalist: And what exactly is it that you do as a digital world designer?

Dr Chang: A digital designer usually **(4)** arranges digital information for companies for different purposes, such as websites or sales promotions. Right now, I am designing digital **(5)** content for a computer game. By the way, in the **(6)** process of production the photos taken in the real world can function as motifs for the animated **(7)** landscapes in the game and mean that I can tailor a virtual reality that is very close to the original.

Journalist: I'm **(8)** intrigued. What is the greatest challenge in projects like that?

Dr Chang: That's a good question. The avatars' mimicry of human **(9)** characteristics such as facial expressions or movements are difficult to create as one is very much aware of them due to our constant need to **(10)** interpret people's body language in our daily encounters. But technology advances quickly and **(11)** facilitates the work in that area.

Journalist: I'm very much looking forward to playing that game. Good luck with the project and thank you for the interview.

Dr Chang: Delighted.

Lösungsvorschläge

Task 1

1. **Journalist:** Dr Chang. Thank you very much for offering the …
   a) ☑ **opportunity** to talk to you […]
2. […] have you always been fascinated by technological …
   b) ☑ **progress**?
3. **Dr Chang:** In the '90s, people started …
   b) ☑ **distributing** information very easily on the internet.
4. A lot of data could be …
   d) ☑ **transferred** from one place to another […]
5. Now, there is a new focus …
   a) ☑ **on** artificial intelligence and all kinds of virtual realities.
6. **Dr Chang:** … their campuses are starting to …
   c) ☑ **attract** graduates who feel an affinity for technology […]
7. You get in touch …
   d) ☑ **with** creative people from all walks of life […]
8. The atmosphere in that area is full of energy and positivity …
   b) ☑ **due to** the rich cultural and diverse spirit of its population.

Task 2

1. qualifications/skills/abilities
2. view/perspective
3. pursue a career/follow a career/be successful/succeed/survive/work
4. test/gain experience in/explore
5. competition/pressure/stress
6. resilience/strength/satisfaction

Task 3

10	2	7	6	4	3
to analyse	Besides	scenery	course	to create	creative ideas

8	0	1	11	5	9
fascinated	dealing	example	to make easier	material	traits

Vocabulary Test 2: Reverse culture shock

(Lebenssituationen, Mobilität in globalisierter Welt, internationale Praktika)

■ *Diese Übung ist genau im Stil der ZP 10 angelegt. Denke an die korrekte Rechtschreibung und Grammatik, damit du die vier Zusatzpunkte erhältst.*

The following text is based on the article "My reverse culture shock: returning from a year abroad is tough. After a life-changing year studying in Canada, coming back home felt like a backward step" by Frances Carruthers.

Fill in suitable words in the correct form or tick (✓) the correct box.

1. Language barriers. Culture shock. Homesickness. These are the things you might ____________________ before departing to study abroad. But for me, returning home proved the hardest of all.

2. After the whirlwind experience of a year abroad – constantly meeting new people, having new experiences and gaining ____________________ – coming home can feel like an anti-climax.

3. Like many other exchange students, I …
   a) ☐ saw b) ☐ took c) ☐ convinced d) ☐ found
   myself living with my parents again after a year in Canada.

4. It felt like I had taken several steps …
   a) ☐ ahead. b) ☐ forward. c) ☐ backwards. d) ☐ around.

5. At first, I indulged in everything I had always ____________________ about being home: days spent lounging with cups of tea and books, tranquil walks and home-cooked dinners. But once the jetlag subsided,

6. I found myself strangely lacking ____________________. I felt constantly restless and slept very little.

7. Why was I feeling so detached? I ____________________ that I had done two things while I was away:

8. I had idealised home in my mind, and I'd expected everything to remain exactly the same while I was away. When I got back and the reality fell short of these ____________________, I experienced what I'd call a reverse culture shock.

9. The idea might seem a bit over the top, especially for exchange students who have only spent a year or less away from home. But as you immerse yourself in a new culture, you quickly …

   a) ☐ accept   b) ☐ adapt   c) ☐ think   d) ☐ reach

   to a different way of life.

10. Meanwhile, everyone at home changes. It was like waking up from a strange dream […]. On top of that, I felt as if I'd changed too. It turns out I wasn't alone: Georgia Zimmer, who studied in France, ____________________ something similar. She says she found herself asking: "How do I fit back into the life I had before when I feel so different? Why is everyone expecting me to be the same as I've always been, when I feel unrecognisable?" […].

11. The feeling of …

   a) ☐ alienation   b) ☐ clash

   c) ☐ stagnation   d) ☐ helplessness

   can be hard to shake off. I kept wondering how long it would take to feel normal again.

12. For Anne Kooijman, returning from Canada to the Netherlands, it was a case of accepting that it would take time, while trying to …

   a) ☐ accommodate   b) ☐ adopt

   c) ☐ integrate   d) ☐ adapt

   some of her new habits and hobbies into her old life.

13. "I am certainly friendlier and less self-oriented, but I am also more open-minded, and want to continue to …

   a) ☐ avoid   b) ☐ experiment with

   c) ☐ challenge   d) ☐ achieve

   doing new things outside of my comfort zone," she says.

14. Getting a part-time job would eventually help ____________________ my own sense of dissociation, as it gave me the structure I needed and the added incentive of earning money. […]

From: Frances Carruthers: My reverse culture shock: returning from a year abroad is tough, abridged: https://www.theguardian.com/education/2017/jul/20/reverse-culture-shock-tough-adjusting-home-studying-abroad (slightly adapted), Copyright Guardian News & Media Ltd 2023

Lösungsvorschläge

1. These are the things you might **worry about/be scared of/be afraid of/fear/expect** before departing to study abroad.

2. After the whirlwind experience of a year abroad – constantly meeting new people, having new experiences and gaining **independence/freedom/self-confidence/new insights** – coming home can feel like an anti-climax.

3. Like many other exchange students, I …

   d) ☑ **found** myself living with my parents again after a year in Canada.

4. It felt like I had taken several steps …

   c) ☑ **backwards.**

5. At first, I indulged in everything I had always **loved/enjoyed/liked** about being home:

6. I found myself strangely lacking **energy/motivation/enthusiasm/inner peace/balance/self-satisfaction**. I felt constantly restless and slept very little.

7. I **realised/noticed/understood/became aware** that I had done two things while I was away:

8. When I got back and the reality fell short of these **ideals/assumptions/memories/dreams**, I experienced what I'd call a reverse culture shock.

9. But as you immerse yourself in a new culture, you quickly …

   b) ☑ **adapt** to a different way of life.

10. Georgia Zimmer, […], **experienced/noticed/felt/realised/reports/went through** something similar.

11. The feeling of …

    a) ☑ **alienation** can be hard to shake off.

12. […] it was a case of accepting that it would take time, while trying to …

    c) ☑ **integrate** some of her new habits and hobbies into her old life.

13. "[…] and want to continue to …

    b) ☑ **experiment with** doing new things outside of my comfort zone," she says.

14. Getting a part-time job would eventually help **ease/deal with/minimise/overcome** my own sense of dissociation […].

Vocabulary Test 3: WWOOFing in New Zealand

(Mobilität in der globalisierten Welt, gesellschaftliches Engagement)

Many young adults don't know what to do after school and take a gap year to find out what they want in their lives. Katie from London is one of them.

Fill in suitable words or tick (✓) the correct box. Give one solution only.

Katie's Travel Blog: First Entry – How it all started … ☺

1. After I had successfully taken my A-levels, I didn't feel quite ready for apprenticeship or ____________________.

2. Honestly, I only had a …

   a) ☐ vague b) ☐ clear c) ☐ slim d) ☐ blurred

   idea of my future career. Also, I had just broken up with my boyfriend after three years of ups and downs in a not very fulfilling relationship.

3. A friend of mine had just returned from a unique ____________________ in New Zealand which made me curious:

4. Louis spent a month working on a remote farm in West Auckland and appeared so […]

   a) ☐ content b) ☐ critical c) ☐ reliable d) ☐ conscious

   and composed that I started doing research on the concept of "WWOOFing".

5. WWOOF is short for 'worldwide opportunities on organic farms' – a global ____________________ with hosts in many different countries.

6. In a nutshell, WWOOFers …

   a) ☐ live b) ☐ manage
   c) ☐ reach d) ☐ spend

   their days some place in the great outdoors and basically learn about agro-ecological methods and sustainability through first-hand experience such as practical gardening or livestock management, i. e. animal care. They are offered food and a place to stay at the farm. In exchange, WWOOFers work on the farm about 6–8 hours, five days a week.

7. Louis, for instance, was …

   a) ☐ accommodated b) ☐ allocated
   c) ☐ given d) ☐ taken

in a simple but clean room with magnificent views of the sea, sky and bush. He rose at 6 o'clock in the morning during the week.

8. Each day he was assigned various manual chores on the farm, for example milking the goats (quite tricky), cleaning up the chicken coop, groundskeeping activities like repairing fences, planting trees and ________________ fruit.

9. I learned that insurance is important for WWOOFers. You don't want to be left sick or hurt or "lose" your property in an unfamiliar place, trying to cover the …

   a) ☐ demands   b) ☐ expenses
   c) ☐ duties   d) ☐ requirements

   or get home without help. Louis explained to me that a WWOOFer is always responsible for his or her own safety.

10. I checked whether or not *my* insurance covers ____________________ including transportation home in case of an accident and dental care.

11. As a WWOOFer you are an independent traveller who is responsible for all travel arrangements and costs (e. g. day trips, internet access), which should be covered by a travel …

    a) ☐ sum.   b) ☐ amount.   c) ☐ budget.   d) ☐ pay check.

12 The idea of escaping city life, creating new connections, learning about ____________________ agriculture and being close to nature as well as the prospect of time for contemplation sounded alluring.

13. Unfortunately, I'm not …

    a) ☐ good   b) ☐ practical   c) ☐ skilful   d) ☐ fluent

    at foreign languages.

14. After a few days of thorough ____________________ and another long talk picking the brains of my friend Louis, I decided to go for New Zealand too. I read that in NZ alone there are about 2,000 hosts and 10,000 WWOOFers. I intended to become one of them!

Curious to learn more about my adventure? Sign up for my blog. I'll keep you posted ☺

Lösungsvorschläge

1. After I had successfully taken my A-levels, I didn't feel quite ready for apprenticeship or **university / college / work / a job**.

2. Honestly, I only had a …

   a) ☑ **vague** idea of my future career.

3. A friend of mine had just returned from a unique **experience / stay / adventure** in New Zealand which made me curious:

4. Louis […] appeared so …

   a) ☑ **content** and composed …

5. WWOOF is short for 'worldwide opportunities on organic farms' – a global **network / community / concept / programme / organisation** with […]

6. In a nutshell, WWOOFers …

   d) ☑ **spend** their days some place in the great outdoors […]

7. Louis, for instance, was …

   a) ☑ **accommodated** in a simple but clean room […]

8. […] groundskeeping activities like repairing fences, planting trees and **harvesting / picking / cultivating / collecting** fruit.

9. […] trying to cover the …

   b) ☑ **expenses** or get home without help.

10. I checked whether or not *my* insurance covers **medical care / medication / medical treatment** including […]

11. […] which should be covered by a travel …

    c) budget.

12 The idea of escaping city life, creating new connections, learning about **regenerative / organic / sustainable / green / eco-friendly / ecological / biological** agriculture and being close to nature […]

13. Unfortunately, I'm not …

    a) ☑ **good** at foreign languages.

14. After a few days of thorough **research / reading** and another long talk picking the brains of my friend Louis […]

Vocabulary Test 4: Veganism in South Africa

(Lebensstile, Konsum und Verbraucherschutz)

Fill in suitable words or tick (✓) the correct box. Give one solution only.

1. JOHANNESBURG – Meat may be meeting its match, as more and more South Africans are ____________________ vegetarian and vegan lifestyles.

2. Veganism – which ____________________ cutting out all meat and products derived from animals, such as dairy, eggs and honey – is slowly growing globally.

3. While there is no official count of how many vegans there are in South Africa, the …

   a) ☐ need b) ☐ claim c) ☐ idea d) ☐ interest

   has led to more and more vegetarian and vegan restaurants in Johannesburg, the nation's economic hub.

4. And this year, Africa's first large-scale vegan and plant-based exposition will ____________________ in Cape Town.

5. Moral and health …

   a) ☐ reasons b) ☐ issues c) ☐ troubles d) ☐ standards

   were cited by many new vegans, like 41-year-old financial adviser Dayalan Nayagar, who made the switch last year after being a lifelong omnivore[1].

6. "I got …

   a) ☐ adapted to b) ☐ integrated into

   c) ☐ known d) ☐ introduced to

   this whole new way of eating, you know healthy, eating organic-type food from plants and I couldn't believe it," he told VOA.

7. "Like I said, it blew my mind and I got fully ____________________ it and I haven't turned back."

8. But, say the owners of one of Johannesburg's hippest, newest vegan eateries, vegans don't have to explain themselves to anyone — though they have been ____________________ doubts and questions.

9. "Where do I even start?" she said. "Someone said I'll definitely die. Very seriously, I have been ____________________ that I will get sick if I continue

to eat this way." Her business partner, Anesu Mbizvo, who is a medical doctor, says science supports a vegan diet. Both women are yoga instructors, and say they feel stronger and better having cut meat from their diet. […]

Meat-based culture

10. But veganism can be a lonely …
    a) ☐ road. b) ☐ concept. c) ☐ activity. d) ☐ hobby.
11. South Africa is the continent's top …
    a) ☐ eater b) ☐ consumer c) ☐ player d) ☐ supporter
    of beef, veal, pork, poultry, mutton and lamb, according to data from the OECD.
12. Many South Africans express horror at the thought of giving up meat, which is central to celebrations and spirituality at family gatherings and celebrations. That's a ____________________ for many African vegans, including Mbviso.

Gradual transition

13. But some South Africans are finding a …
    a) ☐ thoughtful b) ☐ mindful c) ☐ serious d) ☐ crucial
    middle path. Thirty-one-year-old Thandiwe Ngubeni, a communications specialist, still eats meat – but less and less of it as time goes by.
14. "I feel way more energized when I eat a vegetarian or vegan meal," she said, as she eagerly awaited an order of vegan pancakes. "It actually just gives me more ____________________. You don't get that heavy feeling in your stomach."
15. Tseki, a vegan for many years, endorses the slow-and-steady approach. "There's no right way of doing anything," she said. "I think, yes, there are many ____________________ of being vegan. But this is a choice that only you can make."

Abridged and adapted: https://www.voanews.com/a/africa_meet-afri-vegans-south-africa-slowly-embracing-veganism/6182998.html

Annotation

1 **omnivore** – *Allesfresser*

Lösungsvorschläge

1. Meat may be meeting its match, as more and more South Africans are **experimenting with/enjoying/celebrating/interested in/curious about/turning to/adopting** vegetarian and vegan lifestyles.

2. Veganism – which **entails/means/involves/demands** cutting out all meat and products derived from animals […]

3. […] the …

   d) ☑ **interest** has led to more and more vegetarian and vegan […]

4. And this year, Africa's first large-scale vegan and plant-based exposition will **take place/be celebrated/be organised/be held** in Cape Town.

5. Moral and health …

   a) ☑ **reasons** were cited by many new vegans […]

6. "I got …

   d) ☑ **introduced to** this whole new way of eating […]

7. "Like I said, it blew my mind and I got fully **into/involved in/fascinated by/attracted by/immersed in** it and I haven't turned back."

8. […] though they have been **exposed to/confronted with/challenged with/plagued with/deluged with** doubts and questions.

9. "[…] I have been **advised/told/warned** that I will get sick if I […]"

10. But veganism can be a lonely …

    a) ☑ **road.**

11. South Africa is the continent's top …

    b) ☑ **consumer** of beef, veal, pork, poultry, mutton and lamb […]

12. That's a **challenge/problem/loss/sacrifice** for many African vegans […]

13. But some South Africans are finding a …

    b) ☑ **mindful** middle path.

14. "It actually just gives me more **energy/strength/happiness/vigour/power**. […]"

15. "I think, yes, there are many **benefits/advantages/challenges/downsides** of being vegan. […]"

Schreiben

Dieser bedeutende Prüfungsteil macht **insgesamt 60 % des Endergebnisses** der Prüfung aus und ist deshalb besonders interessant.
Du erhältst als **Textgrundlage** voraussichtlich einen literarischen Text (z. B. Auszug aus Roman oder Kurzgeschichte) oder aber einen Sachtext (z. B. Zeitungsartikel). In den letzten Prüfungen wurde stets ein Romanauszug ausgewählt. Das Thema dieses Texts schließt an die Wortschatzaufgabe an. Zum Ausgangstext musst du drei Aufgaben bearbeiten. Dieses Kapitel wird dich Stück für Stück auf die Anforderungen bei allen drei Aufgabentypen vorbereiten.

Bewertungskriterien

Schreibaufgabe (60 % der Gesamtprüfung)	
Inhalt 42 %	
Details dazu siehe unten: „Operatoren und Anforderungen" sowie „Besonderheiten der Aufgabenbereiche"	
Sprachliche Leistung/Darstellungsleistung 58 %	
Kommunikative Textgestaltung	• verständlicher und flüssiger Schreibstil • strukturierte Anordnung der Gedanken • keine unnötigen Wiederholungen von Erkenntnissen • besondere Merkmale der Texte werden berücksichtigt (z. B. bei einer Inhaltsangabe in Aufgabe 1 oder einem Brief in Aufgabe 3 b)
Ausdrucksvermögen und Verfügbarkeit von sprachlichen Mitteln	• Verwendung von eigenen Formulierungen und unterschiedlichen, auch komplexen Satzbaumustern (z. B. mit Relativpronomen – *who, which, that* – oder Konjunktionen – *as, while, if, because* etc.) • angemessener allgemeiner und thematischer Wortschatz, Redemittel der Analyse oder Meinungsäußerung (siehe unten: „Formulierungshilfen")

Sprachliche Korrektheit	Anzahl der sprachlichen Fehler in den Bereichen: • Rechtschreibung und Zeichensetzung • Grammatik (z. B. *tenses, syntax*) • Wortschatz und Ausdruck

Quelle: QUA-LiS, Ministerium für Schule und Bildung des Landes NRW

Bei den Aufgaben im Bereich Schreiben stehen jeweils folgende **Kompetenzen** im Vordergrund:

- Aufgabe 1: Verstehen spezifischer Aspekte des Texts
- Aufgabe 2: Analyse bzw. Interpretation bestimmter Aspekte des Texts
- Aufgabe 3 a): argumentative Auseinandersetzung mit einem spezifischen Aspekt des Texts
  Aufgabe 3 b): kreative, produktionsorientiere Auseinandersetzung mit dem Text

Operatoren und Anforderungen

Die **Aufgabenstellung** ist immer nach dem gleichen Muster aufgebaut und wird mit sogenannten „Operatoren" eingeleitet. Das sind Verben, die deutlich machen, was in der Aufgabe von dir verlangt wird. Dies gibt dir Sicherheit, weil du dich gut darauf einstellen kannst, worauf du dich konzentrieren musst:

Aufgabe	Anforderung & Operatoren/Verben	Gewichtung „Inhalt"
1	Bei allen Operatoren in diesem Bereich geht es darum, bestimmte inhaltliche Aspekte des Texts knapp, sachlich und ohne Wertung wiederzugeben/zusammenzufassen. • ***describe:*** bestimmte Aspekte beschreiben Beispiel: "Describe the situation Sunny is in and how he deals with it." (S. 2022-11) • ***point out:*** bestimmte Aspekte erläutern Beispiel: "Point out the difficulties Gulwali Passarlay faces when he enters university life." (Writing Test 1) • ***summarise:*** die wesentlichen Aspekte zusammenfassen; in einem Einleitungssatz Autor*in, Titel und Thema nennen Beispiel: "Summarise the information given in the excerpt." (Writing Test 4)	ca. 27 %
2	Ein bestimmter inhaltlicher Aspekt wird im Text untersucht oder interpretiert, z. B. durch die Analyse der Erzählperspektive oder der Sprache. Alle Operatoren fordern eine **sachliche Interpretation** bestimmter Aspekte. Jeder Punkt wird mit einem ***topic sentence*** eingeleitet und **am Text belegt**. Du darfst in dieser Aufgabe keine eigene Meinung kundtun.	ca. 40 %

	• ***analyse:*** etwas detailliert erklären und beschreiben Beispiel: “Analyse how Sunny behaves towards Cirrus and how she reacts.” (S. 2022-11) • ***compare:*** die Ähnlichkeiten und Unterschiede zwischen Personen oder Sachverhalten im Detail aufzeigen Beispiel: “Compare the character of the two girls Starr and Kenya considering the point of view in the story.” (Writing Test 3) • ***explain:*** etwas verdeutlichen, indem Begründungen und detaillierte Erklärungen angeführt werden. Beispiel: “Explain what the incident tells the reader about the four boys’ characters. Focus on their behaviour and the way the story is told (narrative technique, use of language).” (Writing Test 4)	
3a) oder	Du kommentierst oder diskutierst einen inhaltlichen Aspekt, der sich aus dem Text ergibt. Bei beiden Operatoren geht es darum, sachlich und höflich zu argumentieren und den Text in Einleitung, Hauptteil und Schluss zu gliedern. • ***comment on:*** den eigenen Standpunkt klar darstellen und mit Begründungen und Belegen/Beispielen untermauern, ein abschließendes Fazit ziehen Beispiel: “Comment on the title of the book ‘The Sound of Silence’”. (S. 2021-11) • ***discuss:*** Pro- und Kontra-Argumente (bzw. Vor- und Nachteile) zu einer Fragestellung klar und mit Begründungen und Belegen darstellen, ein abschließendes Fazit ziehen, das die vorausgehende Argumentation stimmig abrundet. Beispiel: “Discuss the pros and cons of social media platforms.” (Writing Test 2)	ca. 33 %
3b)	Du wirst kreativ und produzierst einen Text, der inhaltlich an den Ausgangstext anknüpft. ***write*** + Textsorte: Hier geht es darum, angegebene inhaltliche Aspekte des Texts aus einem neuen Blickwinkel in einer bestimmten Textsorte sinnvoll abzubilden, z. B. in einem Brief oder einer E-Mail. Dabei musst du die Anforderungen dieser „Zieltextsorten“ genau beachten (z. B. Anrede und Abschluss in E-Mails). Beispiel: “Write a continuation of the story.” (S. 2022-12)	

Quelle: https://www.standardsicherung.schulministerium.nrw.de/cms/zentrale-pruefungen-10/faecher/getfile.php?file=2655

Besonderheiten der Aufgabenbereiche

Vor dem Schreiben: Lies den Text vor der Bearbeitung der Aufgaben mindestens einmal in Ruhe durch, besser zweimal. Schaue dir gerne auch nochmals die Tipps aus dem Kapitel „Leseverstehen" an, die dir hierbei ebenfalls helfen werden.

Aufgabe 1

Diese Aufgabe solltest du auf jeden Fall zuerst bearbeiten, weil du dadurch mit dem Inhalt des Texts noch vertrauter wirst. Wichtig ist, dass du genau das in der Antwort wiedergibst, wonach gefragt wird. Versuche alle diese Aspekte **in eigenen Worten** (meist im *simple present*) präzise zu berücksichtigen bzw. sauber zu formulieren. Ganz wichtig ist, dass in dieser ersten Aufgabe **keinerlei Wertung** vorgenommen werden darf. Interpretiere und kommentiere also nichts!
Nutze eine bestimmte Farbe, um die entscheidenden Infos oder Textpassagen im Text oder am Rand zu markieren.

Aufgabe 2

Schenke dieser Aufgabe strategisch deine größte Aufmerksamkeit, weil sie dir die meisten Punkte einbringt. Hier geht es darum, bestimmte Aspekte im Text zu analysieren und dann auch am Text zu belegen.
Überlege für dich zunächst: Was ist die (versteckte) Absicht oder die Botschaft des Texts? Was passiert gedanklich mit einem Leser oder einer Leserin, wenn er oder sie ihn liest?
Schau dir dann genau die Aufgabenstellung an, die immer ähnlich aufgebaut ist: Vermutlich wirst du aufgefordert, etwas inhaltlich zu erläutern (z. B. das Verhalten einer Person) und dies dann anhand eines Betrachtungsaspekts zu analysieren. Dadurch kannst du die Erkenntnisse deiner Interpretation noch ausschärfen.

Typische Betrachtungsaspekte hierfür sind:
- die **Sprache**, die verwendet wird (Sachtext oder literarischer Text)
- die **Erzählperspektive** (literarischer Text)

Aspekt „Sprache" *(the use of language)*
Wie wird im Text „Sprache" verwendet, um einen bestimmten Effekt in der Leserschaft zu bewirken? Der Betrachtungsaspekt „Sprache" bietet dir sehr vielfältige Möglichkeiten in der Analyse, die nun im Einzelnen aufgefächert werden.

- ***choice of words***
  - Rufe dir das Thema des Texts ins Gedächtnis und überprüfe, ob ein bestimmtes **Themenwortfeld** erkennbar ist oder **Fachbegriffe** (*technical terms* →

scientific character) verwendet werden und ob diese eher positiv oder negativ konnotiert (d. h., „gefärbt") sind.
– Werden viele Adjektive oder Adverbien (sog. ***intensifying adverbs***: *e. g. absolutely, extremely, really*) zur Betonung bestimmter Aspekte verwendet?
– Gibt es bestimmte **Verben**, die verstärkt vorkommen? – z. B., um Ansichten oder starke Emotionen auszudrücken (e. g. *to feel, to cry, to laugh, to shout*)

All dies kannst du in deiner Antwort anführen. Gib dafür, wenn möglich, zwei bis drei Beispiele aus dem Text an und erläutere, welche **Funktion** diese Anhäufung von bestimmten Wörtern hat.

- ***register***
  Welches **Sprachregister** kommt im Wesentlichen zum Tragen? Ist es eher ein gehobenes oder **formales Englisch** *(sophisticated, formal register)*, **Alltagssprache** *(everyday, casual English)*, **Umgangssprache** *(colloquial English)* oder **Jugendsprache** *(teenage slang)*? Welchen Effekt hat dies auf die Leserschaft? Erleichtert die Art der Sprache möglicherweise eine Identifikation? Erscheint ein Autor oder eine Autorin besonders gebildet, glaubwürdig oder überzeugend aufgrund eines gehobenen Sprachstils oder der Verwendung von Fachausdrücken? Wirkt eine Romanfigur sympathisch aufgrund eines lockeren, humorvollen Sprachregisters? Auf solche Aspekte solltest du hier achten.
- ***syntax***
  Wie wird der Satzbau im Text gestaltet?
  – Gibt es bestimmte Muster von Satzstrukturen, z. B. parataktische (aus Hauptsätzen bestehende, oft kurze) Satzstrukturen *(rather short sentences)* oder komplexere (hypotaktische, d. h., aus Haupt- und Nebensätzen bestehende) Satzgebilde *(complex sentence structures)*?
  – Gibt es Wortauslassungen oder unvollständige Sätze *(elliptical sentences)*?
  – Eine Ansammlung von Schlagwörtern? *(an accumulation of key words …)*
  Welchen Effekt löst dies aus? *(The use of paratactical structures adds to the author's/narrator's feeling of … / The use of hypotactical structures gives the text density …)*
- ***imagery, metaphorical language***
  Häufig wird von Autor*innen Bildsprache (z. B. in Form von Symbolen oder Metaphern) verwendet, um etwas besonders anschaulich auszudrücken. Erkennst du einen solchen bildhaften Vergleich, kannst du diesen unter dem Überbegriff „metaphorical language" als solchen kurz erläutern.
  *(This **metaphor** expresses a strong feeling of…/emphasises … / The dove is a **symbol of** peace./The dove stands for peace.)*

Die Sprachanalyse kannst du in **Writing Tests 1, 2** und **4** trainieren.

TIPP Achte in der ZP 10 genau darauf, ob der Aspekt „Sprache“ in der Aufgabenstellung genauer eingegrenzt wird, z. B. durch „choice of words“. Dann musst du dich natürlich darauf konzentrieren.

Aspekt „Erzählperspektive“ *(narrative technique)*

Zunächst unterscheidet man zwischen **Autor*in** (also einer real existierenden Person) und **Erzählinstanz** *(narrator)* eines literarischen Werkes. Dabei gibt es den ***first-person narrator*** oder den ***third-person narrator***. Bei beiden Erzählformen gilt es zusätzlich den *point of view*, also die Perspektive eines Charakters, aus der berichtet wird, zu erkennen.

- ***First-person narrator***
  Hier wird stets aus der Ich-Perspektive berichtet, häufig aus der der Hauptfigur, manchmal wechselt die Perspektive aber auch zwischen unterschiedlichen Charakteren. Dies hat zur Folge, dass man als Leser*in womöglich nur Zugang zur Gedankenwelt der Hauptfigur hat und sich dadurch ggf. besser mit ihr identifizieren kann, weil man nur *ihre* Beweggründe kennt und die Geschehnisse aus *ihrer* Sicht an einen herangetragen werden *(limited point of view)*.
- ***Third-person narrator***
  Bei dieser Erzählform kann es ebenfalls sein, dass nur die Perspektive einer Figur eingenommen wird *(limited point of view)*. In diesem Fall gelten im Grunde die gleichen Konsequenzen für die Möglichkeit der Identifikation wie bei einem *first-person narrator*.
  Oder aber der *third-person narrator* steht außerhalb der Geschichte und hat Zugang zur Gedanken- und Gefühlswelt aller oder mehrerer Charaktere innerhalb der Geschichte *(omniscient point of view)*. So kann in der Leserschaft der Eindruck entstehen, dass die Geschehnisse „objektiver“ geschildert oder präsentiert werden und eventuell findet eine differenziertere Betrachtung oder gar Abgrenzung zu Verhaltensweisen von Charakteren statt.

In der Analyse wird oft erwartet, dass man inhaltlich etwas in der Szene erläutert und zudem analysiert, um welche Erzählform und Perspektive es sich handelt und welche Konsequenzen dies wiederum auf die Leserschaft hat. In **Tests 1, 3** und **4** kannst du die Analyse der Erzähltechnik üben und an Beispielen nachvollziehen.

Arbeit mit Textbelegen bzw. Zitaten

In der Analyse solltest du deine Aussagen immer am Text belegen. Dies kannst du tun, indem du z. B.

(1) ein kurzes Zitat oder einen prägnanten Begriff aus dem Text in einen eigenen Satz von dir einbaust.

(2) bei Bedarf Auslassungen in Zitaten oder kleine Veränderungen mit eckigen Klammern kenntlich machst.

(3) lediglich auf ein oder mehrere Textpassagen in Klammern verweist. Dafür kannst du die Abkürzung „cf.“ (dt. „vergleiche“) verwenden.
(4) einen ganzen (meist) kurzen Satz nach einem Komma/Doppelpunkt zitierst.
(5) ein kurzes Zitat in Klammern hinter einem Satz von dir einfügst.

Im folgenden Beispiel kannst du die möglichen Vorgehensweisen im Kontext nachvollziehen (vgl. auch Writing Test 3):

> (**1**) The reader learns about her character that she is not interested in fancy party dressing and wears her brother's "oversized hoodie" (l. 35). (**2**) She is "feeling basic [...] with [her] ponytail" (ll. 15/16), which contrasts (**3**) Kenya's bouncing curls (cf. l. 5) and the other girls' refined hairstyles (cf. l. 15).
>
> (**4**) Star appears quite self-confident on the outside when she provocatively asks Kenya, "Do I look like I care what people think?" (l. 42).
>
> (**5**) In addition, she is quick-witted and ironic in some moments ("I didn't know so many mind readers live in Garden Heights," l. 24).

Aufgabe 3 a)

Du verfasst eine **Diskussion** oder einen **Kommentar** zu z. B.

- einem Zitat aus dem Text,
- der Meinung eines Journalisten oder einer Journalistin in einem Artikel oder der Figur in einem literarischen Text,
- einer Problemfrage, die im Text direkt oder indirekt thematisiert wird,
- einer herausfordernden Situation aus dem Ausgangstext.

In einer **Diskussion** bist du aufgefordert, **beide** Seiten (**Pro** und **Kontra**) mit Argumenten und Beispielen abzuwägen und dann für dich ein Fazit zu ziehen. In einem **Kommentar** wird erwartet, dass du klarer z. B. zu einer Konfliktfrage Position beziehst. In beiden Fällen spielt es keine Rolle, welche Position du selbst hast, entscheidend ist vielmehr die Qualität deiner Argumente und ein sachlicher Stil. Überlege dir auch gerne einen griffigen Titel bzw. eine Überschrift für deinen Text.

Aufgabe 3 b)

Bei dieser Art von Aufgabe sollst du an den Text anknüpfen und kreativ selbst einen Text produzieren, z. B. aus einer anderen Perspektive. Dies kann sein:

- eine E-Mail, ein Erfahrungsbericht, ein Tagebucheintrag, ein Blogeintrag, ein (in)formeller Brief, ein Leserbrief,
- ein alternatives Ende zu der Romanszene, die dir vorliegt,
- die Fortsetzung der Romanszene.

Du bekommst hier zusätzliche inhaltliche Hinweise („Include the following aspects“), die du berücksichtigen sollst. Sie helfen dir bei der Entwicklung weiterer Ideen und bei der Struktur deines Texts. Beginne immer mit einem Brainstorming und notiere dabei zusätzliche Aspekte, die du im Text geschickt einbauen kannst.

Formulierungs- und Strukturhilfen

Summary

- *The text (excerpt) taken from the novel/newspaper article … written by … was published in … and deals with …*
- *The contents of the excerpt/article can be summarised as follows: …*

Analysis

Die folgende Tabelle kannst du bei Bedarf beim Verfassen von verschiedenen Analysen (insbesondere zu Romanauszügen) zur Unterstützung heranziehen: Sie bietet dir Aufbau- und Strukturhilfe, Hinweise zu den einzelnen Textbausteinen sowie etwas textanalytisches Vokabular zur Auswahl.
Die 2–3 Sinnabschnitte im Hauptteil werden vorzugsweise mit einem *topic sentence* eingeleitet. Du kannst ihre Reihenfolge natürlich verändern.
Deine Analyse solltest du stets im Präsens verfassen.

introduction (introduce thesis)	
In your introduction, you can mention the topic of the literary excerpt and you outline your general **thesis** regarding the task.	• In the literary excerpt/article, the author mainly deals with … In the following, the … will be analysed/explained/compared closely. • In addition, narrative techniques employed in the text and/or the author's use of language will also be focused on.
main body (prove thesis)	
# paragraph 1 **Focus of analysis** You start the paragraph with a topic sentence, in which you say what you will be elaborating on contentwise: in your first paragraph you generally analyse the **content** in detail in accordance with the focus of the task.	• topic sentence: The subject of …/conflict between …/the character(s) … is/are presented/portrayed/depicted as complex/twofold/divisive/one-dimensional/troubling/provocative/particularly interesting etc.

You **explain** certain aspects (e. g. a form of behaviour, conflict, relationship) by referring to text passages that prove your findings.	• Having a closer look at …, one can say / conclude / expect / claim … • Besides, when …, it becomes obvious that … • On the one hand …on the other … • To put it in a nutshell, …
# paragraph 2 **Narrative perspective / Point of view** Then you examine the point of view and explain how it helps to • portray a certain character / situation / conflict • create a certain effect for the reader Don't forget to **quote** from the text and give examples.	• <u>topic sentence</u>: Narrative techniques also help to portray … (a conflict / person / relationship) • The novelist, XY, uses of a first / third-person narrator (with a limited / omniscient point of view). The events are shown from XY's perspective. • Consequently, the reader can(not) identify with … / understands … / relives the situation through XY's eyes …
# paragraph 3 **Use of language** Now, you analyse aspects of language, e. g. the **choice of words, register, sentence structure or metaphors** and explain their possible effects on the reader. Again, **quote** from the text. Use appropriate quoting techniques.	• <u>topic sentence</u>: Not only does the author use narrative techniques to … but (s)he also uses a certain kind of language to depict / illustrate … • The author's register is everyday English / formal / poetic /sophisticated / scientific etc. to appear trustworthy / educated / credible etc. to the reader. • This is (also) reflected by his / her choice of words which … / The choice of words gives the text a rather … tone. • The vocabulary contains many … expressions relating to the word field … • The repetition of the word "…" (l. xy) emphasises … • Moreover, XY's use of language supports the idea that … • In addition, the metaphor in line XY suggests that …
conclusion	
final words (on thesis) End your text by referring to your introduction and formulating a **concluding sentence** in which you briefly refer to your ideas in the main body of the text again. Do <u>not</u> make any personal comments on the quality of the literary excerpt.	• Taking a closer look at the beginning / introduction of the analysis, one can conclude that … • All in all, the author uses different strategies to … • Above all, his / her … and … help him / her to … • To sum up, …

Personenbeschreibung

- *The protagonist/principal character/main character in the story is …* – Die Hauptfigur ist …
- *Another central character is …* – Eine weitere zentrale Figur ist …
- *As to her social position, one can say that …* – Was ihre soziale Position betrifft, kann man sagen, dass …
- *As far as his/her character is concerned/Concerning his/her character …* – Was seinen/ihren Charakter betrifft …
- *to have an aggressive temperament/bad character* – ein aufbrausendes Temperament/einen schlechten Charakter haben
- *to have many positive character traits/characteristics/personality traits* – viele positive Charaktereigenschaften haben
- *His/Her predominant character trait is …* – Sein/Ihr vorherrschender Charakterzug ist …
- *Another essential quality is …* – Eine weitere bedeutende Eigenschaft ist …
- *His/Her behaviour/conduct is marked by arrogance/selfishness/fear/naivety etc.* – Sein/Ihr Verhalten ist geprägt von Arroganz/Selbstsucht/Angst/Naivität … usw.
- *His/Her conduct is mainly influenced by …* – Sein/Ihr Verhalten ist hauptsächlich beeinflusst von …
- *He/She considers him-/herself (to be) inferior/superior to others* – Er/Sie betrachtet sich anderen gegenüber als unter-/überlegen …
- *to have a deep mistrust of sth* – ein tiefes Misstrauen gegenüber etwas haben
- *to react indifferently to …* – gleichgültig reagieren auf …
- *to show great sensitivity* – große Sensibilität zeigen

Letter – E-mail – Letter to the editor – Diary

Beginning:

- *Dear Dad*
- *Dear Ms/Mrs/Mr Smith*
- *Dear Sir or Madam* (wenn du den Namen der Person nicht kennst)
- *Dear Diary*

End:

- *Please give my regards to …* – Bitte richte … Grüße von mir aus.
- *I'm looking forward to hearing from you soon.* – Ich freue mich darauf, bald von dir zu hören.

Formal letter/e-mail:
- *Yours sincerely* (wenn du den Namen der Person kennst)
- *Yours faithfully* (wenn du den Namen nicht kennst)
- *Kind regards* (etwas weniger formell)

Personal letter/e-mail:
- *Love* (wenn du die Person sehr gut kennst und ein sehr vertrautes Verhältnis besteht)
- *Yours* (neutraler)

Letter to the editor:
Achtung: Die Person, an die du schreibst, ist nicht der oder die Autor*in. Der Leserbrief richtet sich vielmehr an die Redaktion bzw. den Herausgeber, die für die Veröffentlichung zuständig sind (passende Anrede: *Dear Sir or Madam*).
- *I am writing in response to the article "…" in …* – Ich beziehe mich auf den Artikel „…" in …
- *The author conveys the impression that …* – Der Autor/Die Autorin vermittelt den Eindruck, dass …
- *I strongly disagree with …/disapprove of …* – Ich lehne … entschieden ab/missbillige …
- *I approve of/I agree with …* – Ich befürworte/bin einverstanden mit …
- *to call sth into question* – etwas in Frage stellen
- *In my opinion/view* – Meiner Meinung nach
- *Unlike the author, I hold the position that …* – Im Gegensatz zum Autor/zur Autorin bin ich der Meinung, dass …
- *to distance oneself from sb/sth* – sich von jmd./etwas distanzieren
- *to have reservations about sth* – Vorbehalte gegenüber etwas haben
- *To my knowledge …* – Nach meiner Kenntnis …
- *Let's not forget that …* – Lasst uns nicht vergessen, dass …

Discussion/Comment

introduction
- *It is true that …* – Es stimmt, dass …
- *It goes without saying that …* – Es versteht sich von selbst, dass …
- *It stands to reason that …* – Es liegt nahe/auf der Hand, dass …
- *At first glance, one might feel inclined to support/oppose …* – Auf den ersten Blick mag man geneigt sein … zu unterstützen/abzulehnen.

main body
- *I'll begin with …* – Ich beginne mit …
- *First of all, …* – Zuallererst …

- *The question arises as to why ...* – Es stellt sich die Frage, warum ...
- *It is essential that ...* – Es ist unerlässlich, dass ...
- *Supposing that ...* – Angenommen, dass ...
- *It is true that ..., but strictly speaking, ...* – Es ist richtig, dass ... aber genau/streng genommen ...
- *This seems to be true, but in fact ...* – Das scheint zu stimmen/zuzutreffen, aber in Wirklichkeit ...
- *I do not intend to ..., but ...* – Ich habe nicht vor ..., aber ...
- *On the one hand ... on the other hand ...* – Auf der einen Seite ..., auf der anderen Seite ...
- *Additionally/Furthermore/Moreover* – Darüber hinaus/Außerdem/Zudem
- *As a consequence/Consequently* – In der Folge/Folglich

Conclusion
- *In summary/In conclusion/In a nutshell* – Zusammenfassend lässt sich sagen
- *On the whole/Generally speaking* – Im Großen und Ganzen/Insgesamt
- *So, one thing is certain:* – Eines ist also gewiss/sicher:
- *I would like to conclude that ...* – Ich möchte abschließend feststellen, dass ...

Grundsätzliche Strategien, Tipps zur Vorbereitung im Schulalltag

Bei dieser Aufgabe gilt ganz besonders: Übung macht den Meister! Je häufiger du diese Aufgaben konzentriert im Unterricht und bei der Vorbereitung zu Hause trainierst, desto schneller, effektiver und erfolgreicher wirst du sie in der Prüfung bewältigen. Die Erfahrung zeigt, dass Lernende, die Übungsangebote im Unterricht hierzu annehmen und daheim in Ruhe trainieren, wenig Schwierigkeiten mit dieser Aufgabe haben und nicht in Zeitnot geraten.
Zudem helfen auch v. a. die Tipps aus den Kapiteln „Leseverstehen“ und „Wortschatz“ in diesem Buch.

Writing Test 1: Migration to the UK

(Migration und Mobilität, soziale/politische Teilhabe, Berufsorientierung)

Text **The lightless sky** by Gulwali Passarlay

After his father's death, Gulwali Passarlay was sent away from Afghanistan at the age of twelve as a so-called child refugee. He made terrible experiences on his dangerous migrant journey to Britain, which took him about one year. In the UK, Gulwali was taken care of by a foster family, went to school and won a place at a top university. In the following excerpt, he describes some of his experiences at university.

In 2013, all my hard work paid off and I won a place at Manchester University. Walking through the grounds on my first day was quite possibly the happiest I had been in my life. I couldn't stop smiling as I queued to get my ID card; I don't think I have ever been so excited to be in a long line of people all shuffling forward at a snail's pace.

At the front of the queue were tired-looking administration staff sitting behind computers finalizing the enrolment for each student.

I passed the time thumbing through my papers, which I otherwise kept pressed to my chest in a manila folder, as if someone, or something, might steal them away. Part of me felt like an imposter[1], as if at any moment I might be unmasked as a fraud and ignominiously marched from[2] this elite institution.

"Name?" asked a round-faced woman, without looking up.

"Gulwali Passarlay. I am studying politics. It's so–"

"Parsley?"

I laughed. "It's a bit difficult to spell …"

At school I had known everybody's face, if not their names; here I was a tiny cog[3] in a huge machine. The lecture theatres held hundreds of students, so I would try to arrive early to get a good seat. I loved the specialist classes[4]. It felt as though my educational journey had exited the broad motorway of core learning. Now I travelled the path I wanted to take. My mind was opened to people, places and experiences I never could have imagined. The academic rigour[5] tested my brain until it hurt. I also loved the tutorials, where we would discuss and debate politics, domestic and foreign, past and present, until the tutor[6] forced us out of the door when the class time expired.

Essays were another matter. My written English was still developing, so I found them extremely challenging. I struggled to articulate what was so clear in my head.

When I wasn't at my classes, or studying in the library, I often relaxed by people watching. As an Afghan I'm no stranger to tribalism[7], and at Manchester University it was alive and thriving. Some students congregated[8] along ethnic lines. Some, notable for their insistence on dressing entirely black, were united in a love of a certain style of music. Other musical tribes draped themselves in American sporting apparel and baseball caps. A few clumped together according to sexuality and fiercely stood their ground amid the freedom of thought and experience fostered by the university.

This was very new to me, but I taught myself to keep an open and inquiring mind whenever I felt culturally challenged by anything.

And I had been in the UK long enough by now to have learned to love the general culture of tolerance.

My own tribe was a long, long way away, but I carried their memory with me everywhere. Sometimes I wished I could have shown my mother around university. She would have been astonished and proud of how far her little boy had come. And the look on her face when she saw how some of the other students dressed would have been priceless.

From: Gulwali Passarlay, Nadene Ghouri, The Lightless Sky – My Journey To Safety As A Child Refugee, *Atlantic Books, London 2015, pp. 352–354*

Annotations

1 **imposter** – faker
2 **ignominiously marched from** – strictly banned from
3 **cog** – tiny wheel
4 **specialist classes** – refers to courses the author attends at university
5 **rigour** – strictness
6 **tutor** – a teacher at university
7 **tribalism** – being organised in and feeling loyal to peer groups
8 **to congregate** – to meet

Tasks

- *Read the tasks carefully.*
- *Make sure to write about* ***all*** *the aspects presented in each task.*

HINT Start by analysing the tasks carefully. Usually you are told to focus on certain aspects, which is a guideline for both the expected content of your answer and the structure of your text. To help you with this analysis, the key words are already underlined in this first writing test.

1. **Point out** the difficulties Gulwali Passarlay faces when he enters university life.
2. **Analyse** the protagonist's various emotions during his first semester at university. Look at how the events are told (narrative technique and use of language).
3. Here you can choose between two different options.

option a)

Discuss the benefits and challenges of studying in a foreign country.

Include the following aspects in your text:
- financing and accommodation,
- various intercultural and emotional situations,
- your future job prospects.

OR

option b)

After his first semester at Manchester University, Gulwali **writes a letter** to his mother about his experiences at the institution.

Write that letter and include the following aspects:
- his fears, hopes and expectations at the beginning of the term,
- his perception of university life in Britain (e. g. classes and students),
- three questions he asks his mother in Afghanistan.

HINT In tasks 3 a) and b) you always get some help with the aspects to focus on. The three bullet points after "include the following aspects" could be the starting point for your brainstorming. They also give you an idea of how to structure your letter.

Lösungsvorschläge

1 **HINT**

Lies den Text einmal für einen ersten Überblick und sammle beim zweiten Lesen dann stichpunktartig alle Herausforderungen, denen Gulwali sich stellt. Manche springen einem womöglich schneller ins Auge als andere.
Wichtig ist beim Operator „point out", dass du eine knappe Erläuterung ergänzt.
Folgende **Schwierigkeiten** werden im Textauszug direkt oder indirekt benannt:

- *difficulty for some people to understand his Afghan surname "Passarlay"*
- *Gulwali is not used to the mass of students in the institution: anonymity*
- *high academic level challenges him intellectually: problems with written English as a refugee speaking and learning a foreign language*
- *culturally unfamiliar with a variety of lifestyles reflected by diverse groups of students*
- *feeling of loneliness/sadness, as separated from home country and mother*

In the excerpt taken from his autobiography *The Lightless Sky*, Gulwali Passarlay mentions several problems at university, which will be pointed out in chronological order. (introductory sentence)

First, some people might have difficulty understanding his name, as Gulwali has to spell his Afghan surname to a seemingly unfriendly clerk when he enrols at the administration office. (challenges at university)

Second, Gulwali is not used to the mass of students on campus which leads to an anonymous atmosphere in a way he did not experience at school.

One serious obstacle is his written English, which Gulwali is eager to improve but which particularly challenges him when it comes to writing academic essays.

Gulwali also sets foot in new territory interculturally when he gets to know the various lifestyles of diverse groups of students from all walks of life.

At the end of the excerpt, he brings up the distance to his home country and his mother, whom he misses and would like to show around.

2 **HINT**

Sieh dir bitte auch die Tabelle zur Struktur einer Analyse zu Beginn des Kapitels an (Abschnitt „Formulierungs- und Strukturhilfen"). Diese kannst du gut für alle Analyseaufgaben nutzen.
Die Aufgabenstellung zeigt dir, dass du den Hauptteil dieser Analyse am besten in drei Abschnitte unterteilst: *Analyse the protagonist's various emotions* (**1**) *during his first semester at university. Look at how the events are told – narrative technique* (**2**) *and use of language* (**3**).

Die Analyse-Aufgabe in dieser Übung ist sehr komplex, weil du aufgefordert bist, ...

- ... inhaltlich unterschiedliche **Gefühle** des Protagonisten zu analysieren (**1**)
  - *dominant/prevailing emotion from first day onwards: complete happiness and excitement (cf. ll. 1–5)*
  - *peculiar feeling of fear of not being accepted/losing privileges ("imposter", l. 10), feeling lost, anonymity (ll. 16–18)*
  - *pride ("elite institution", l. 11; "my mother [...] would have been astonished and proud", ll. 40/41)*
  - *love of the different classes and tutorials he attends (ll. 18–24)*
  - *ambition/impatience (struggles with language, eager to make progress, cf. ll. 25/26)*
  - *sometimes feels "culturally challenged" (l. 36): Gulwali is taken by surprise by the diverse range of people that come together*
  - *feeling of sadness/loneliness indirectly expressed when he thinks about his "own tribe" (l. 39) being far away and his mother*
- ... die Auswirkungen der **Erzählperspektive** in diesem Kontext zu berücksichtigen (**2**)
  - *first-person narration, autobiography → the fact that a real person is offering insight into his thoughts and feelings might particularly arouse the reader's curiosity*
  - *honest, sensitive and modest reporting of events and inner life → likeable narrator → identification possible, particularly for other (foreign/refugee) students*
- ... **sprachliche Aspekte** zu untersuchen, die helfen, diese Emotionen abzubilden (**3**)
  - *superlative → one of the "happiest" days of his life (l. 2)*
  - *(repetition of) positive, strong, expressive verbs reflecting dominant emotion of happiness (e. g. "smiling", l. 3; "to love", ll. 18, 22) and adjectives ("happiest", l. 2; "alive and thriving" l. 29)*
  - *contrasted with verbs and adjectives expressing his difficulties (e. g. "hurt", l. 22; "challenging", l. 26; "struggled", l. 26; "challenged", l. 36)*

- *intensifying adverb to emphasise his feelings ("extremely", l. 26)*
- *adjectives ("challenging", l. 26; "new" l. 35; "inquiring" l. 35) express the constantly difficult process of learning/adapting on different levels (academic competence, culture, language)*
- *metaphorical language: "I was a tiny cog in a huge machine" (ll. 16/17) → lack of individuality, feeling of being somewhat lost; "exited the broad motorway of core learning" (l. 19) → feels happy and overwhelmed by the speed of making his own specific choices in terms of education*

Versuche in deiner Analyse, die für dich aussagekräftigsten Erkenntnisse zu bündeln, ggf. neu zu ordnen und dabei Textbelege anzuführen (Hilfe zum Zitieren findest du ebenfalls zu Beginn des Kapitels, Abschnitt „Arbeit mit Textbelegen bzw. Zitaten"). Die folgende Musteranalyse ist zur Anschaulichkeit besonders ausführlich gestaltet. Bestimmte Erkenntnisse, die zuvor beim Brainstorming zum Aspekt Sprache gefunden wurden, werden im Text aber bewusst nicht mehr verwendet: Konzentriere dich stets auf das Wichtigste.

introduction: thesis

In the literary excerpt taken from the autobiographical novel *The Lightless Sky*, the author and first-person narrator, Gulwali Passarlay, mainly outlines his impressions and emotions during his first semester at university.
In the following, these feelings will be analysed in detail. In addition, the effect of narrative techniques employed in the text and the author's use of language will also be focused on with regard to the narrator's emotional rollercoaster.

main part: emotions

topic sentence

Gulwali experiences a range of complex emotions, such as happiness, excitement, anxiety, confusion and homesickness, as he navigates his new academic environment.

→ happiness, excitement

From his first day onwards, a mixture of complete happiness and sheer excitement prevails as he considers entering university life as of one of the "happiest" (l. 2) moments in his life and he cannot "stop smiling" (l. 3). Furthermore, when he speaks about his classes and tutorials, it becomes obvious that he enjoys them very much and is "proud of how far [he] ha[d] come" (l. 41) because he is part of an "elite institution" (l. 11).

→ pride

→ vague feeling of fear and insecurity

However, on taking a closer look at the beginning of the excerpt, one could say that Gulwali is also troubled by an underlying fear of not being accepted and of being excluded because of his imagined lack of competence, as he admits, "[p]art of me felt like an imposter" (l. 10). He struggles with writing in English, and feels "culturally challenged" (l. 36), as he is often taken by surprise by the diverse range of people that come together.

Gulwali indirectly expresses his sadness and loneliness when he thinks about his "own tribe" (l. 39) being far away and his mother, whom he would like to show around.
To put it in a nutshell, his life at university is shaped by happiness, excitement, curiosity and the willingness to adapt and work hard.

→ sadness, loneliness

Narrative technique also helps to illustrate the emotional portrayal of Gulwali's first semester. It is quite rare for the author and the first-person narrator to be one and the same. As the events are shown from a real person's perspective, the reader may be inclined to sympathise with the honest excitement, curiosity and challenges described in the excerpt.
Consequently, students in general and students with an immigrant or refugee background in particular can identify with Gulwali when they relive the situation through his eyes.

narrative technique
topic sentence

Not only does the author employ narrative techniques to depict his various emotions but he also uses descriptive language to paint a picture of his physical and emotional state.
His choice of words, which is dominated by positive verbs ("smiling", l. 3 and "to love", ll. 18, 22, for example) and adjectives ("happiest" l. 2, "alive and thriving" l. 29), gives the excerpt a rather optimistic tone. This spirit and the great opportunity to shape one's own curriculum are also conveyed metaphorically: "[i]t felt as though my educational journey had exited the broad motorway of core learning. Now I travelled the path I wanted to take" (ll. 18–20).
The repetition of the word "love" (ll. 18, 20) emphasises Gulwali's overall appreciation and happiness.
However, adjectives like "challenging" (l. 26) or "inquiring" (l. 35) promote the idea of the constant challenges he faces as a migrant student, such as the language barrier or a different cultural background.
To sum it all up, the use of language also primarily reflects Gulwali's cheerfulness.

language
topic sentence
choice of words
→ positive verbs and adjectives
metaphorical language
repetition
contrast: adjectives expressing difficulties

Taking a closer look at the beginning of the analysis, one could conclude that Gulwali manages to cope with a complex set of emotions in his first semester. He uses different strategies to enable the reader to understand them by offering direct access to his inner thoughts and using descriptive language with sensitivity.

conclusion

3 **HINT** **option a)**

In dieser Aufgabe geht es im Grunde darum, Vor- und Nachteile eines Studiums im Ausland in einer gewissen Balance abzuwägen.
Du solltest hier auf jeden Fall die drei in der Aufgabenstellung vorgegebenen Punkte *(financing/accommodation, intercultural/emotional situations, job prospects)* in deinem Text berücksichtigen. Du kannst diese noch durch eigene Gedanken (auch inspiriert durch den literarischen Text) anreichern, z. B.:

Benefits	***Challenges***
• *enriching cultural immersion/ enhancement of intercultural* competence (people, traditions etc.) • *making new friends* • *foreign language acquisition/ improve language skills* • *new career opportunities/ international networking* • *personal growth: self-confidence/ independence/self-organisation*	• *financial burdens (e. g. tuition fees, higher rent, expensive food, travel* expenses) • *visa, legal issues, insurance* • *language barrier* • *intercultural challenges/ embarrassments (e. g. lifestyle, customs, values)* • *homesickness*

Studying in another country can be a valuable and rewarding opportunity. However, there are also obstacles to consider before you decide to take that step.

introduction – topic of discussion

It goes without saying that enriching your intercultural competence is one of the greatest benefits, as living in a foreign country allows you to experience a new culture and different way of life, which can broaden your horizons and help you become more open-minded. You will be inspired by interesting people with different mindsets, backgrounds and traditions. It is a wonderful opportunity to make new friends and create long-lasting bonds that are precious.

main part: benefits
→ intercultural competence, inspiration, networking

Moreover, studying in a foreign country is an excellent opportunity to improve your language skills, whether you are learning a new language or improving your proficiency in one.

→ language skills

The last advantage I would like to focus on is that studying abroad can open up new career opportunities and improve your chances of success in the global job market when you enter the world of employment. Potential employers will appreciate your experiences and may conclude that you are more independent, confident and adaptable than other candidates.

→ job prospects

However, there are also challenges involved in studying in a foreign country, including the language barrier: even if you are studying in a country where you speak the language, you may still have difficulty understanding lectures, completing assignments and communicating with the locals.

challenges
→ language barrier

You might also consider that being away from your friends and family for an extended period of time may be difficult and could lead to feelings of homesickness, which can be aggravated by moments of culture shock. Adjusting to a new culture can be challenging and may take some time. In addition, you may unintentionally make an intercultural faux pas in various communicative situations.

→ emotional distress, intercultural challenges

Last but not least, studying abroad can be expensive in terms of living expenses (food and accommodation, for example) and may require you to take on additional financial responsibilities or navigate various legal requirements (a visa, for instance).

→ financial burden, legal issues

Overall, studying abroad can be a valuable, rewarding and unforgettable experience, but it also requires careful planning and meticulous preparation to ensure that you are able to handle the challenges that come with it.

conclusion

HINT **option b)**

Politische Hintergrundinfo zu Afghanistan im Jahr 2013:
Im Jahr 2013 waren die Taliban ***nicht*** an der Macht. Eine afghanische Regierung handelt zu dieser Zeit mit den USA ein Sicherheitsabkommen aus, um die militärische Präsenz von US-Truppen in Afghanistan weiter aufrechtzuerhalten.

Tipps zur Aufgabe:
Begebe dich empathisch in die Situation von Gulwali im Jahr 2013 und verfasse aus seiner Sicht (u. a.) zu den geforderten Punkten einen Brief. Formulierungshilfen und Tipps zu Briefen findest du übrigens zu Beginn des Kapitels.

Es empfiehlt sich, den Textausschnitt mehrfach zu überfliegen und Informationen zu den drei Spiegelpunkten der Aufgabe zu markieren und in der gegebenen Struktur zu sammeln, z. B.

- ***his fears, hopes and expectations*** *as a refugee at the beginning of the term*
  - *fears: not being accepted, not being prepared/ready; expulsion*
  - *hopes: to live up to/fulfil/meet academic demands, meet new people, focus on favourite choices in terms of classes, tutorials, study groups*
  - *expectations: academic degree, further cultural immersion, language acquisition*

- ***his perception of university life in Britain*** *(e. g. classes and students)*
  - *atmosphere of respect and tolerance; challenging and inspiring at the same time*
  - *very new impressions: different kinds of people in terms of lifestyle, religion, sexual identity, ethnic background etc. → lively discussions about politics, society, history, tradition and culture*
- ***three questions he asks his mother*** *in Afghanistan, e. g. about*
  - *a possible reunion one day in the UK or Afghanistan*
  - *the family situation (e. g. health of relatives and friends, everyday life)*
  - *the political situation at home: Afghan government; US and NATO troops in the country*

Dear Mother, — address

I hope this letter finds you well. — **introduction**

main part

I would like to share with you my experiences so far at Manchester University. To be honest, I don't know where to start …

fears, hopes, expectations

When I first arrived, I was filled with joy, fear and uncertainty. On the one hand, I worried about fitting in and being accepted as a migrant student. Would I live up to the high academic standards?

On the other hand, I was thrilled and looking forward to finally making my own choices in terms of university classes and topics for writing essays.

As the semester went on, I found that my hopes and expectations were exceeded.

university life in Britain

University life in Britain has been quite different from what I had imagined and feared.

The classes are challenging but engaging, and the professors are knowledgeable and supportive.

I particularly enjoy the lively conversations about politics and foreign affairs, which have really broadened my horizons.

I think I will be able to succeed in obtaining my degree if I keep up the hard work.

My fellow students are diverse and come from all over the world, which has made my experience even more enriching, even though I sometimes feel lost in the crowd.

The atmosphere of respect and tolerance is challenging and inspiring at the same time for a person from a very different cultural background. But I'm eager to learn and have made good friends I can talk to and confide in.

You would be astonished to see what campus life is like in the UK.

I have a few questions for you, if you don't mind. How is everyone at home? Are you well? questions

What is your everyday life like now? Have things changed a lot?

And how is the situation in Afghanistan? Do you feel safe?

I miss you all and think of you often. My hope is that we can reunite in some way soon.

I am grateful for the opportunity to study here and am excited to see what the future holds.

Please send my love to everyone in the family. **closing**

Love,

Gulwali name

Writing Test 2: Social media addiction

(Bedeutung digitaler Medien für den Einzelnen und die Gesellschaft)

Text **I deleted my social media apps because they were turning me into an idiot** by Lydia Smears

Giving up Facebook and Instagram made me realise I was using them to block out real emotions with likes. But I couldn't help going back.

In January I deleted all the social media apps from my phone because they were turning me into an idiot.

For months I'd been avoiding engaging with anything challenging or anxiety inducing. Worried about where I'd be living next year? Dive into Instagram. Tax bill prickling at the back of my mind? Open Facebook. That grief I thought I'd processed piercing at me again? Disappear into the realm of likes and follows and push the feelings away. Distract. Binge. Escape.

Whether it was the Pavlovian[1] thrill of the little red circles of like notifications, or a genuine need to connect with others, there was something that kept me – along with 1.86bn other active monthly Facebook users – going back. With social apps so accessible on my smartphone, this had turned into compulsive checking. Statistica[2] research shows that 47% of UK adults use social media every day, and a GlobalWebIndex[3] report found that at the end of last year people were spending a global average of almost two hours a day on social and messaging networks. I was one of them.

Hours of my evenings, train journeys and lunchtimes were spent hopping from one app to another, cruising for attention in the form of likes. I'd open Facebook, then Instagram, then Messenger, and in the time it had taken me to look at the latter two there was a chance that something might have happened on Facebook. So back I'd go and open it again. Then Instagram. Then Messenger. The cycle would continue. It was annoying the hell out of me. It wasn't even meaningful attention I was seeking – if social media wasn't forthcoming, I'd dip into work email, or even my banking app, in the hope of finding something new there. I just craved something – anything – in the form of a new notification. I felt like a frantic lab rat waiting to hear a bell ring. […]

So I went clean. I took them all off my phone. […] After I deleted Facebook, Twitter and Instagram from my phone, I was alarmed at the amount of free time that suddenly emerged. I used to think I was way too busy to read these days. But within a month I'd read two novels and listened to an audio book. […] In the moments before bed, while waiting for my boyfriend to finish brushing his teeth, rather than checking Instagram, I put a drawing pad and pencil on my bedside table to sketch out photo ideas. Beyond this, I also found that in moments of boredom,

I'd text or email friends or relatives I hadn't spoken to for a while. I even phoned some people for a catch up, which felt weird at first. […]

I would like to say that, the cycle broken, I let the apps back into my life but only to use occasionally, for wholesome purposes, while continuing to nurture off-line relationships and reading lots more. But it's hard to manage the pull of compulsive checking. […] It worries me that these networks encompassing everyone I know provide empty, addictive rewards for pointless behaviour. And it worries me that as long as I have a phone in my pocket, that scrolling idiot I'm capable of being is only ever a few clicks away.

From: Lydia Smears: I deleted my social media apps because they were turning me into an idiot, https://www.theguardian.com/technology/2017/mar/14/deleted-social-media-apps-facebook-instagram-emotions-likes (9. 2. 22), Copyright Guardian News & Media Ltd 2023

Annotations

1 **Pavlovian** – Allusion to Ivan Pavlov, a Russian psychologist famous for classical conditioning and his experiments with dogs

2 **Statistica** – Statistica offers a range of analytics software which can be used to analyse, classify and visualise data.

3 **GlobalWebIndex** – British company studying digital consumerism

Tasks

- *Read the tasks carefully.*
- *Make sure to write about **all** the aspects presented in each task.*

HINT Again, you should start by analysing the tasks carefully by highlighting key words that give you guidance for your answers, for example. Have a look at the tasks from Writing Test 1 again if you need some help finding key words.

1. **Describe** the problems the author had as well as her immediate plan of action to solve them.
2. **Analyse** the language she uses to put forward her message about social media usage. Focus on choice of words, comparisons and syntax.
3. Here you can choose between two different options.

option a)

Discuss the pros and cons of social media platforms.

Include the following aspects:

- the quality of information posted,
- the impact on its users,
- personal observations or experiences in your everyday life with digital media.

OR

option b)

Imagine you're a student counsellor with a blog for young people in trouble. You read about Lydia Smears' experience. **Write an article for your blog** about the sensible use of social media platforms in life as a teenager.

Include the following aspects:

- a catchy headline and a subheading providing information on the subject,
- observations or experiences in your everyday life with digital media,
- ideas on how to deal with the problems caused by digital consumerism.

1 **HINT**

Die Aufgabenstellung besteht aus zwei Teilen (was man an folgenden *key words* erkennt: *problems, plan of action*) und entsprechend sollte der Antworttext konzipiert werden.

Zuerst eine **Aufzählung der beschriebenen Probleme**:

- *neglected serious tasks and obligations in everyday life, avoided coping with negative emotions*
- *clung to her smartphone constantly*
- *addiction to digital world/activities: constant checking for messages, e. g., on Twitter or Instagram*
- *led to a lack/absence of true emotions*

Dann die Angabe, **wie die Autorin für sich das Problem gelöst hat**:

- *(digital) detox: she deleted all social media apps from her smartphone and found time to engage in different activities, only used apps to maintain or revive deeper personal relationships*

In her online article in *The Guardian*, the author, Lydia Smears, realises that she avoided serious obligations and challenges in her everyday life (paying bills, for example) and indulged in the digital world with her smartphone instead to distract herself on Facebook or Twitter. She used social media to avoid coping with negative emotions. introductory sentence problems

She developed a serious addiction, constantly checking if there were new messages on Instagram, for example.

She realised that she had stopped experiencing real emotions and decided to solve the problem by radically deleting all the apps that had kept distracting her. She then found time to occupy herself with different activities like drawing, reading or getting in touch with friends (again). immediate plan of action to solve problems

2 **HINT**

Folgende Vorgehensweise und Struktur erscheinen sinnvoll für diese Analyse:

1. Überlege zunächst, was die **Botschaft** *(key word: message)* von Lydia Smears ist. Was möchte sie den Leser*innen mitteilen?

- *a friendly appeal or warning to create a healthy balance between "real" life and (toxic/harmful) virtual activities → emotional stability*
- *indirect suggestion to evaluate your own consumption of digital/social media activities in a constructive, critical and honest manner*

2. Überprüfe dann, wie die Autorin **Sprache** *(key word: language)* benutzt, um dies zu erreichen. Konzentriere dich dabei auf …
   - die **Themenfelder** im Wortschatz und die Auswahl bestimmter Verben sowie (optional) darüber hinaus den **grundsätzlichen Ton** des Texts, der ebenfalls durch die Wortwahl deutlich wird:
     - *choice of words is marked by numerous movement verbs reflecting her constant and hectic use of social media apps ("dive", l. 4; "disappear", l. 6; "hopping", l. 16; "cruising", l. 17)*
     - *semantic field of negative emotions and addiction displaying her addictive behaviour in terms of social media use ("anxiety", l. 3; "grief […] piercing at me", ll. 5/6; "compulsive", l. 11; "craved", l. 24; "I went clean", l. 26; "addictive rewards", l. 39)*
     - *optional: generally casual and sometimes colloquial and humorous tone/style of writing reveals that she is just one of many people dealing with the problem ("turning me into an idiot", headline/l. 2; "I was one of them", ll. 14/15; "It was annoying the hell out of me", l. 21) → identification; defusing effect*
   - einige bildhafte bzw. prägnante **Vergleiche**, die du gut erklären kannst:
     - *comparisons metaphorically illustrating her addiction and loss of control over herself, which she ultimately regains ("I felt like a frantic lab rat waiting to hear a bell ring", ll. 24/25; "Pavlovian thrill […] little red circles", l. 8; "The cycle would continue", ll. 20/21 – "the cycle broken", l. 35)*
     - *personification of her apps ("I let the apps back into my life", l. 35) → dominance in her life*
   - den besonderen Einsatz von bestimmten **Satzbaumustern** im Text. Frage dich dabei, warum die Autorin diese Sätze bewusst so gestaltet hat.
     - *use of paratactic/cryptic sentence structure emphasising her permanent feeling of restlessness and the inner urge to go online: series of short, elliptical questions and answers (cf. ll. 4–7); "Distract. Binge. Escape." (l. 7); "Then Instagram. Then Messenger." (l. 20)*
3. Überlege dir schließlich eine schlüssige Struktur. Dabei kann es sinnvoll sein, bei der Dreiteilung *(choice of words, comparisons, syntax)* zu bleiben. Genauso stimmig kann es aber sein, etwas zu mischen und sprachliche Phänomene zu bündeln, die ähnliche Effekte bei der Leserschaft erzielen.

introduction: thesis with message

In her online article, Lydia Smears appeals to the reader in a friendly way to create a healthy balance between their "real" everyday lives and harmful activities in the digital world. She is worried that digital networks "encompassing everyone" (l. 38) result in "pointless behaviour" (l. 39) in too many people's lives. Her article is a wake-up call or even well-intended warning for people to critically evaluate their own use of social media to preserve or regain emotional stability. To achieve this, she uses convincing strategies language-wise, which will be analysed in the following paragraphs.

main part: use of language

→ choice of words

The first focus is on her choice of words. The author makes particular use of movement verbs that reflect her constant and hectic use of social media apps ("dive", l. 4; "disappear", l. 6; "hopping", l. 16; "cruising", l. 17). The semantic word field of addiction demonstrates her addictive and manic behaviour in terms of social media use. She uses words and phrase like "anxiety" (l. 3), "grief […] piercing at me" (ll. 5/6), "compulsive" (l. 11), "craved" (l. 24), "I went clean" (l. 26), "addictive rewards" (l. 39).

→ tone of the text

→ personification

In addition, a humorous and sometimes colloquial tone ("idiot", l. 2; "I was one of them", ll. 14/15; "It was annoying the hell out of me", l. 21) creates a defusing effect and puts the reader at ease and the personification of the apps (cf. l. 35) makes the reader smile.

Therefore, readers are willing to connect with the approachable and likeable person she seems to be or even identify with some of her experiences when they catch themselves doing the same thing.

→ comparisons, metaphorical language

Some very strong images illustrate the author's loss of control over herself very well as Lydia Smears compares herself to a "frantic lab rat" (ll. 24/25), probably with "red circles" (l. 8) in her eyes, constantly eager for notifications of almost any kind (cf. ll. 21–24). She admits having being caught in a destructive "cycle" (l. 20) which she was unable to escape. Some readers will be familiar with that vicious cycle and are left thinking about it.

→ syntax

Smears' skilful use of parataxis and sometimes even cryptic, elliptical sentence structure also adds to the overall picture of a woman troubled by the permanent feeling of restlessness and the inner urge to go online (cf. ll. 4–7, l. 20).

conclusion

All in all, one could say that Lydia Smears skilfully applies various strategies in terms of language to illustrate her struggle and put forward her message to develop a more balanced use of social media apps and step back into the "real" world if necessary. The reader is left thinking about their own media consumption and might consider going on retreat just like her.

3 **HINT** **option a)**

In dieser Aufgabe geht es darum, Vor- und Nachteile von sozialen Medien in einer gewissen Balance abzuwägen. Du solltest hier auf jeden Fall die drei Spiegelpunkte der Aufgabe (vgl. fett gedruckte Punkte in der Tabelle) in deiner Diskussion berücksichtigen und kannst diese noch durch eigene Gedanken (bei den „cons" auch inspiriert durch den Artikel) anreichern, z. B.:

Pros	***Cons***
• ***quality of information posted*** *reliable sources (e. g. expert opinion) can broaden your horizons/ be a help at school* • ***impact on its users*** *wise and thoughtful ideas from reasonable people can influence, reach and inspire an international audience* • ***personal observations or experiences in your everyday life with digital media,*** *e. g. …* – *people belonging to a minority can connect easily with peers and find support* – *healthy balance: real-life activities (e. g. sports, meeting friends offline) vs. virtual activities (e. g. meeting friends online)* – *effective strategies for monitoring your own daily or weekly screen time and social media activities*	• ***quality of information posted*** *fake news, deep fake, anonymity, various illusions/questionable ideals, hate speech and cyberbullying are serious problems to address* • ***impact on its users*** *users may be misled, badly influenced, follow false role models, be hurt* • ***personal observations or experiences in your everyday life with digital media,*** *e. g. …* – *the conditioned reflex to check messages or to scroll as a distraction → waste of time* – *privacy breaches* – *the impact of cyberbullying on victims (e. g. depression)* – *the pressure to live up to standards/ideals propagated by influencers in their peer groups*

introduction

In my everyday life with digital media, I have observed that social media can be both a positive and negative force.

main part: pros

Empowered by media literacy, social media allow people to share knowledge and creative ideas, and access news and information from a variety of reliable and trustworthy sources. In fact, wise and thoughtful input from reasonable and well-educated people can reach, influence and inspire an international audience in a positive way.

You can instantly rely on expert opinions online and do research for school projects, for example.
Moreover, you always have platforms for immediate connection with your friends and family.
If you happen to belong to a minority in terms of your cultural background, religion or sexual identity or if you are simply interested in a particular hobby, you can easily connect with your peers in your region or internationally on social media, find support or engage in the same (outdoor) activity.
As long as you have been trained in assessing and scrutinising online information and you have developed a healthy balance between real life events and online activities, social media can be very beneficial.

On the other hand, I have also seen how social media can be used to spread misinformation in political campaigns, for example, perpetuate cyberbullying and harassment in classrooms, and generally have a negative impact on mental health. Social media platforms are regularly misused for privacy breaches. cons
One should also consider the questionable ideals propagated by some famous influencers and the illusions they create, which may put pressure on young people who fail to live up to those standards.
Additionally, the urge to check your smartphone apps permanently needs to be monitored and handled sensibly. Sometimes, you may catch yourself scrolling pointlessly for information like a frantic lab rat …

In a nutshell, it is important for individuals to use social media responsibly and for wholesome purposes and to be aware of the potential negative effects it can have. **conclusion**

HINT **option b)**

Übernehme hier die Perspektive eines Coaches, der*die täglich mit Herausforderungen von Jugendlichen im Umgang mit sozialen Medien konfrontiert wird und diese jungen Menschen sensibel und lösungsorientiert berät. Gestalte so kreativ einen Blogeintrag, der dir vor allem beim zweiten und dritten Punkt Raum für eigene Ideen bietet. Versuche auch den Stil eines Blogbeitrags zu treffen, indem du z. B. durch Zwischenüberschriften, Aufzählungen und kurze Absätze für Übersicht und leichte Lesbarkeit sorgst. Idealerweise kommt in diesem Kontext auch noch zwischen den Zeilen heraus, dass man sich bei Bedarf bei einem Coach Hilfe suchen könnte.

- ***title & subheading***
  - *think of a catchy or interesting title and provide more information in the subheading*
- ***observations or experiences in your everyday life with digital media**, e. g.:*
  - *the danger of fake news, privacy breaches and cyberbullying causing distress among teens*
  - *false role models and propagated ideals putting pressure on young adults*
  - *development of addiction resulting in excessive screen time*
- ***ideas on how to deal with the problems caused by digital consumerism**, e. g.:*
  - *careful monitoring of screen time (on social media) with the help of parents/friends*
  - *meaningful use of social media*
  - *comparison trap: question and disregard so-called ideals, concepts and standards set by some influencers*
  - *digital detox/breaks from social media → regular exercise, (outdoor) activities with "real" friends, family etc.*
  - *seek (professional) help and support if necessary*

Mind the Trap! 5 Tips for Finding Balance in a Digital World: The Benefits of Mindful Social Media Use for Teens — heading

Empowering young people to make healthy choices in a connected world — subheading

As a student counsellor, I have seen the impact that social media and technology can have on the mental health and well-being of young people. — introduction to the topic

In today's world, we are constantly connected. We wake up and check our phones, scroll through our timelines throughout the day and wind down with a few more hours of screen time on social media before bed.

While we do so, we are exposed to the dangers of privacy breaches, fake news and cyberbullying. — dangers of social media use

The constant connectivity and exposure mentioned above can lead to feelings of anxiety, failure by comparison and even addiction.

But it doesn't have to be that way.

Here are five tips for healthy social media use: — how to deal with problems caused by digital consumerism

1. **Set limits:** Decide on a specific amount of time to spend on social media each day and stick to it. Use apps that help track your usage and set reminders to log out.

2. **Be intentional:** Use social media for a purpose, such as staying connected with friends and family or following accounts that inspire or educate you. Avoid aimlessly scrolling for hours on end.
3. **Mind the comparison trap:** Social media can be a breeding ground for comparison and self-doubt. Remember that people often create illusions and only post their highlights. Try to focus on your own life and goals.
4. **Take breaks:** Take time away from social media, even if it's just for a few hours or a day. Use that time to connect with friends and family, to exercise or to pursue other hobbies in the "real" world.
5. **Seek help:** If you find yourself feeling overwhelmed or addicted to social media, don't hesitate to reach out to a trusted friend, family member, teacher or counsellor for support.

By making conscious choices about our social media use, we can closing
reduce its negative impact on our lives and find balance in a connected world. By being mindful, we can use technology for the good and lead happier, healthier lives.

Writing Test 3: Growing up and fitting in

(Alltag und Freizeit, Lebensstile in der peer group, *Jugendkulturen)*

Text — **The Hate U Give (excerpt)** by Angie Thomas

The following text is taken from the first chapter of the novel The Hate U Give. *The protagonist, Starr Carter, is 16 years old and lives in a poor American neighbourhood called Garden Heights. Unlike her peers, Starr goes to an elite high school in a different part of the city.*

I shouldn't have come to this party.

I'm not even sure I belong at this party. That's not on some bougie[1] shit, either. There are just some places where it's not enough to be me. Either version of me. Big D's spring break party is one of those places.

I squeeze through sweaty bodies and follow Kenya, her curls bouncing past her shoulders. A haze lingers over the room, smelling like weed, and music rattles the floor. Some rapper calls out for everybody to Nae-Nae[2], followed by a bunch of "Heys" as people launch into their own versions. Kenya holds up her cup and dances her way through the crowd. Between the headache from the loud-ass music and the nausea from the weed odor, I'll be amazed if I cross the room without spilling my drink.

We break out the crowd. Big D's house is packed wall-to-wall. I've always heard that everybody and their momma comes to his spring break parties – well, everybody except me – but damn, I didn't know it would be this many people. Girls wear their hair colored, curled, laid, and slayed. Got me feeling basic as hell with my ponytail. Guys in their freshest kicks and sagging pants grind so close to girls they just about need condoms. My nana[3] likes to say that spring break brings love. Spring in Garden Heights doesn't always bring love, but it promises babies in the winter. I wouldn't be surprised if a lot of them are conceived the night of Big D's party. He always has it on the Friday of spring break because you need Saturday to recover and Sunday to repent.

"Stop following me and go dance, Starr," Kenya says. "People already say you think you all that.[4]"

"I didn't know so many mind readers live in Garden Heights." Or that people know me as anything other than "Big Mav's daughter who works in the store." I sip my drink and spit it back out. I knew there would be more than Hawaiian Punch in it, but this is way stronger than I'm used to. They shouldn't even call it punch. Just straight-up liquor. I put it on the coffee table and say, "Folks kill me, thinking I know what I think."

"Hey, I'm just saying. You act like you don't know nobody 'cause you go to that school."

I've been hearing that for six years, ever since my parents put me in Williamson Prep[5]. "Whatever", I mumble.

"And it wouldn't kill you to not dress like." She turns up her nose as she looks from my sneakers to my oversized hoodie.

"That. Ain't that my brother's hoodie?"

Our brother's hoodie. Kenya and I share an older brother, Seven. But she and I aren't related. Her momma is Seven's momma, and my dad is Seven's dad. Crazy, I know. "Yeah, it's his."

"Figures. You know what else people saying too. Got folks thinking you're my girlfriend."

"Do I look like I care what people think?"

"No! And that's the problem!"

From: Angie Thomas, The Hate U Give, *Harper Collins Publisher, USA 2017, pp. 3–6*

Annotations

1 **bougie** – bourgeois, fancy, here: arrogant
2 **Nae-Nae** – hip hop dance
3 **nana** – grandma
4 **you think you all that** – you think you are better than us
5 **Williamson Prep** – wealthy, majority-white private school

Tasks

- *Read the tasks carefully.*
- *Make sure to write about* ***all*** *the aspects presented in each task.*

1. **Describe** the setting and the atmosphere.
2. **Compare** the character of the two girls Starr and Kenya considering the point of view in the story.
3. Here you can choose between two different options.

option a)

At the end of the excerpt Starr asks Kenya, "Do I look like I care what people think?" – (l. 42)
Comment on Kenya's reaction: "And that's the problem!" (l. 43)

Include the following aspects:
- the challenge for teenagers like Kenya and Starr to find their identity
- the importance of trends and other people's opinion in life as a teenager
- how much you should adapt to your social environment or its expectations

OR

option b)

Later on, Kenya **writes a series of text messages** to a friend and reports on the party as well as Starr's behaviour.

Write those messages and include the following aspects:
- how she perceives the atmosphere at the party
- her opinion of Starr
- her hopes and fears at Big D's house

1 **HINT**

Die Aufgabe besteht wieder aus zwei Teilen:

Setting (place and time)

Action takes place at a spring break party in the house of someone called 'Big D' in the American neighbourhood of "Garden Heights" on a Friday in spring, probably sometime in the 2000s to 2010s.

Atmosphere

- *crowded, noisy, hot, joyful/wild, but also sombre/negative vibe*
- *the house is crowded with a large number of people and it seems to be very hot inside the rooms*
- *Most guests (except for Starr) are carefully styled according to the current teenage fashion trends. → excessive dancing and listening to loud rap music*
- *there is hardly enough space to make your way through the crowd*
- *boys and girls are flirting, chatting and dancing very close to each other*
- *some party guests are smoking weed*
- *a lot of alcohol is drunk*
- *optional: negative vibes: protagonist Starr feels like an outsider (cf. l. 2), conflict between Starr and Kenya (cf. ll. 22/23, 42/43)*

In the excerpt taken from the opening chapter of the novel *The Hate U Give* by Angie Thomas, the story is set at a spring break party in the house of someone called Big D in the American neighbourhood of "Garden Heights" on a Friday. The action probably takes place in the 2000s or early 2010s. introductory sentence setting

The atmosphere at Big D's party can be described as crowded, noisy and a bit wild or even excessive. The house is full of a large number of people, who (except for Starr) are carefully styled according to the current teenage fashion trends. They are dancing and listening to very loud rap music. There is hardly enough space to move around and it is very hot as the people are sweating. Boys and girls are flirting, talking and dancing very close to each other. Some party guests are smoking weed and the guests are drinking a lot of alcohol. atmosphere

As well as the joyful party atmosphere there are also negative vibes as Starr, the protagonist of the story, feels out of place at the party and gets into an argument with another girl, Kenya.

2 **HINT**

Hier geht es um einen Vergleich von zwei Charakteren unter Berücksichtigung der Erzählperspektive, die natürlich einen Einfluss darauf hat, was und wie etwas berichtet wird. Diesem Umstand sollte bei der Bearbeitung besondere Beachtung geschenkt werden. Hier empfiehlt es sich deshalb sogar, mit der Klärung der Perspektive zu beginnen.

Narrative technique, point of view

- *first-person narrator – Starr's point of view (limited) → reader has access to her inner thoughts and feelings.*
- *information on Kenya is less profound as only delivered in Kenya's direct speech and Starr's descriptions of her and direct comments to her*

Comparison

- *Starr and Kenya are related in a peculiar way as they "share an older brother" (l. 37), but seem to be very different in terms of their character*

Starr

- *self-confident ("Do I look like I care what people think?" l. 42)*
- *quick-witted, ironic ("I didn't know so many mind readers live in Garden Heights", l. 24; "Folks kill me, thinking I know what I think", ll. 28/29)*
- *does not seem to fit in, feels uncomfortable – clearly not interested in wild parties, loud rap music or excessive dancing ("headache", l. 9; "I shouldn't have come", l. 1)*
- *does not dress like the other girls in terms of hair or clothing: wears "sneakers" (l. 35) and her brother's "oversized hoodie" (l. 35)*
- *people believe she feels superior to them because she goes to "that school" (l. 31)*
- *inner conflict: "[e]ither version of me" (l. 3) → hybrid identity as she is part of two worlds: the elite school and the poor neighbourhood (cf. introduction to excerpt)*

Kenya

- *happy to be at the party where she dances her way through the crowd (cf. ll. 8/9)*
- *wants to make a good impression ("go dance, Starr", l. 22), does not want to stand out from the crowd, very concerned about "what people think" (l. 42)*
- *clearly annoyed by Starr's attitude and rumours about Starr being her girlfriend; feels uncomfortable in her presence ("Stop following me", l. 22)*
- *does not want to be seen with Starr, who is considered arrogant and a lesbian ("Got folks thinking you're my girlfriend", ll. 40/41)*

At the start of the opening chapter of the novel, the author, Angie Thomas, starts painting quite a complex picture of the protagonist Starr Carter, whereas the reader only gets a vague idea of Kenya, the other character in the scene.

introduction
thesis

This is due to the fact that the story is told by a first-person narrator who relates the action from Starr's perspective only. As a reader, one has access to her inner thoughts and feelings. Information on Kenya is therefore less detailed, and is delivered in Kenya's direct speech and, above all, Starr's descriptions of her and direct comments to her.

maint part: point of view

The two teenage girls are related in a peculiar way as they "share an older brother" (l. 37) but seem to be very different in terms of their character. Even though they are growing up in the same poor neighbourhood, Starr goes to Williamson Prep, a private school outside the area.

general comparison of both characters

As a consequence, Starr appears to be quite different from Kenya. She does not seem to fit in at the party and feels uncomfortable. She clearly is not interested in wild parties or loud rap music. The atmosphere gives her a "headache" (l. 9) and right at the beginning she realises that she "shouldn't have come to this party" (l. 1). It becomes obvious that she has developed some kind of hybrid identity, being part of both Garden Heights and Williamson Prep, as she refers to two "version[s]" of herself (l. 3) and wonders where she belongs (cf. l. 2). The people in her neighbourhood falsely assume that she feels superior to them because she goes to "that school" (l. 31).
The reader learns that she is not interested in dressing up for parties and wears her brother's "oversized hoodie" (l. 35) and "sneakers" (l. 35). Her simple "ponytail" (l. 16) stands in stark contrast to Kenya's bouncing curls (cf. l. 5) and the other girls' polished hairstyles (cf. l. 15).
Starr appears quite self-confident on the outside when she asks Kenya provocatively, "Do I look like I care what people think?" (l. 42). In addition, she is quick-witted and ironic in some moments ("I didn't know so many mind readers live in Garden Heights", l. 24, for example).

Starr

Unlike Starr, Kenya is happy to be at the party, where she easily dances her way through the crowd (cf. ll. 8/9), and wants them to make a good impression ("go dance, Starr", l. 22). Kenya is clearly annoyed by Starr's non-conformist attitude and rumours about Starr being her "girlfriend" (l. 41). She feels uncomfortable in her presence ("Stop following me", l. 22) and does not want to be seen with Starr, who is considered arrogant (cf. ll. 22/23) and a lesbian ("Got folks thinking you're my girlfriend", ll. 40/41).

Kenya

In contrast to Starr, Kenya cares a great deal about what other people think and believes that Starr's refusal to fit in is "the problem" (l. 43).

Considering the point of view and comparing the behaviour of the two girls at the party, the reader draws the conclusion that the girls' characters are quite different: Starr appears to be a witty and complex loner troubled by the balancing act of navigating two environments, whereas Kenya fits into the party scene and is very much aware of the crowd's opinion of them. **conclusion**

3 **HINT** **option a)**

In einem Kommentar bist du aufgefordert zu einem Sachverhalt nach Abwägung bestimmter Argumente Position zu beziehen. Wie siehst du also den Spagat im Leben junger Menschen, einerseits Erwartungen ihres Umfelds Genüge zu tun und, andererseits, sich selber treu zu bleiben? Sammle zunächst Ideen zu den drei angegebenen Punkten, z. B.:

Challenge for teenagers like Kenya and Starr to find their identity
- *rocky path for teenagers navigating different environments: peers at school, family, teachers, society, norms, set standards and values*
- *Starr: overwhelmed by challenge; admiration for her distancing herself from party scene – price she pays?*
- *Kenya: rather shallow, pressure to be accepted*

Importance of trends and other people's opinion in life as a teenager
- *peers/close friends – people you can really trust and who know and like who you truly are*
- *role models (relatives, friends, artists, teachers etc.)*
- *pick the right ones, those you can really look up to in terms of talents or values*

How much you should adapt to your social environment or its expectations
- *find the middle path to get along*
- *Starr: troubled by negative feelings/thoughts bugging her*
- *Where is your safe haven?*

Who am I? Who am I Gonna Be? – Being Comfortable on that Journey

heading (optional)

Starr's statement "Do I look like I care what people think?" (l. 42) suggests a disregard for the opinions of others, and Kenya's response, "And that's the problem!" (l. 43) implies that this attitude is problematic. But that is rather black and white, is it not? **introduction:** subject matter

The argumentative dialogue between Starr and Kenya shows that it is particularly challenging for teenagers to navigate a rocky path in different environments in the process of finding their identity. Who are you going to listen to? Your peers at school, your parents, your teachers, opinionated members of society who comment on current norms, values and set standards you need to observe? That can be very complex, unnerving and confusing.

main part: challenges to find one's identity

At this stage of life, it is common for individuals to be heavily influenced by trends and the opinion of their peers. While it is important for teenagers to be true to themselves, it is also necessary to understand that social dynamics and expectations do play a role in shaping your identity. True friends that really accept you the way you are and whom you can confide in can be your rock. They can help you find the right role models to be inspired by.

importance of trends and other people's opinions

Starr, like many young adults in real life, is torn between two worlds which do not seem to complement each other. She struggles and has decided to question the common rules for parties and people's reputations, whereas Kenya seems to represent those teenagers that willingly adapt to expectations and common stereotypes and do not want to stick out of the crowd.

Starr and Kenya (how much adaptation is "right"?)

Starr's and Kenya's circumstances and their dispute show that, ultimately, finding a healthy balance between staying true to yourself with the help of friends and the right role models and connecting with your social environment a little at the same time can be a way to strike a happy balance between developing your individuality and being respectful of the people around you.

conclusion: balance between adaptation and individuality

HINT option b)

Hier sollst du dich in die Perspektive von Kenya hineinversetzen und, kreativ mit eigenen Gedanken angereichert, eine Reihe von Textnachrichten verfassen. Sieh dir noch einmal an, was du in der Analyse über sie herausgestellt hast. Überlege anschließend, welches Sprachregister sich für Kenya anbietet und wie du realistisch und gleichzeitig fantasievoll eine Textfolge gestalten kannst.

Mögliche Stoffsammlung:

How she perceives the atmosphere at the party

- *she likes the atmosphere: cool music, relaxed, happy people, interesting conversations, excessive dancing, great drinks, cute guys*
- *some people staring at her and Starr, strange looks, some party guests are looking at Starr's outfit*

Her opinion of Starr

- *she dresses in a rather sloppy and boyish manner – provocation?*
- *she wants to show that she, a student at Williamson Prep, is better than the rest*
- *Starr clings to her like a limpet* (dt.: wie eine Klette an jdm. hängen)
- *Kenya respects Starr's sense of humour and self-confidence*
- *Kenya envies Starr's opportunity to go to an elite school*

Her hopes and fears at Big D's house

- *fears that people will spread the rumour that she and Starr are a couple*
- *hopes to meet this cute guy she met at the last football game where she was cheerleading*

Hey there … address

I was so looking forward to going to that party. I wore that new hot dress and it took ages to get my hair ready. I just loved the atmosphere at Big D's house: cool music, relaxed, happy people, interesting conversation, dancing, great drinks and … cute guys!!! 😎 atmosphere at the party

Unfortunately, I couldn't get rid of Starr. She kept following me around ALL THE TIME. 😒

What is wrong with that girl? Coming to a party in our brother's oversized hoodie??? Not doing her hair?? Can you imagine the looks … people staring at her sloppy, boyish outfit? And that constant depressing, condescending look on her face? opinion of Starr

Why can't she at least pretend to have a a good time … pay more attention to current trends? Why did she even come if it's not her thing? Everyone knows Big D's parties are kind of excessive 😉

Why is she that provocative all the time? Why does she want to stick out? I don't get it, really. Everyone already knows she goes to Williamson Prep. I'd love to go there too, I have to admit. I admire her for being a smartass in the right situations in a way. She's not one to be bossed around. She helped me with my ex-boyfriend once, remember … And, yeah, she has kind of a good sense of humor. We can talk to each other and are somehow related and all but I had to find a way to stop her clinging to me like a limpet at the party.

I don't want the rumor to spread any further that we're together. That really bugs me 'cause I'm not gay. Don't get me wrong. One of my favorite cousins is gay. I once joined a meeting at the LGBTQ club at school, remember? fears

But Tyson, the guy I met at the football game, wanted to go to the party too. 😍 I thought we could have some fun …, get to know each other. hopes
Being called a lesbian wouldn't help me there …

Kenya XXX closing

Writing Test 4: Bullying at school

(Lebenssituationen, Jugendkulturen, Einblicke in den Schulalltag)

■ *Trigger-Warnung: Der folgende Text enthält Szenen, in denen es zu Gewalt gegen ein Mobbing-Opfer kommt.*

Text **The Pōrangi Boy (excerpt)** by Shilo Kino

The following text is taken from the beginning of the novel The Pōrangi Boy*: Twelve-year-old Māori Niko lives in Pohe Bay: a (fictional) small, rural town in New Zealand. Right now, he is at school.*

'Pōrangi[1] boy, I know it's you!'

I recognise Kaore's ugly voice and picture his stubby fingers rattling the door. I look up at the ceiling, wondering if I can escape through the tiny window just above the toilet. Nah, probably not.

I jump down to the ground, throw my bag over my shoulder and push the door open, ready to do a runner.

Tū, Kaore and Hone are standing in front of me. Tū's got a big smirk on his face. He nods slightly and Kaore lifts me up by my bag and shoves me against the toilet.

'Tsk tsk, boy,' Tū says. 'You reckon you can hide from us, aye?'

'What do you want?' I ask, rubbing my head.

Tū's eyes narrow and he grabs my bag and tips it upside down. Pens, scrunched-up paper and a packet of Twisties[2] fall out.

'Oh, yo!' Hone says and snatches at the Twisties like it's the first time he's ever seen food.

'What's that over there?'

'Noth–'

Tū picks up the book Miss Martin gave me. '*Matilda,*' he says.

They all look at each other and crack up like it's the funniest thing in the world.

Tū throws me back on the floor and drops the book into the toilet. It makes a splash before it bobs up and down in the water.

'You better get your book.'

I bend over to scoop it up, trying not to put my hand in the mimi water for too long.

Suddenly, my arms and legs are jerked from behind.

'Let me go!' I try to swing my arms, but Kaore and Hone are holding on to both of them.

'How does it feel to have no one liking you, pōrangi boy?'

Tū pulls down his zipper and starts pissing in the toilet.

I'm pushed back and my head's dunked into Tū's piss. A gush of water swirls around. The toilet flushes and my head is yanked back up. I gasp for air, coughing and spluttering. They all start cracking up. I feel a kick to my back. Hone chucks the empty Twisties packet at me and then they disappear.

I shake my hair and quickly wrap the book in lots of toilet paper. The pages are soggy and it smells. I grab my bag and walk outside.

A hand touches my shoulder. Miss Martin's big blue eyes are staring into mine. She looks me up and down. 'Oh geez, what happened to you?'

'Nothing, Miss,' I say, trying to pretend my hair isn't drenched in piss.

She screws her face up but still looks pretty.

'Those boys been picking on you?'

'What boys?'

She gives me a look. 'Don't you let those boys push you around, Niko.'

'I don't, Miss.'

'What did they do?'

'Nothing, Miss.'

She raises her eyebrow. 'What's that?'

I glance down at my hands. *Matilda*'s wrapped up in toilet paper.

I quickly hide it behind my back.

'Nothing.'

She fiddles in her bag and pulls out a set of keys. 'You come see me at the library if you ever need a place to hang out, okay? I'll see you tomorrow.'

'See ya! Miss.'

Her ponytail swings back and forth as she walks to her car.

She's humming a song, probably Taylor Swift. She presses a button on her keys and hops into her little red car.

From: Shilo Kino: The Pōrangi Boy; *Huia Publishers, Wellington NZ 2020, pp. 2/3*

Annotations

1 **pōrangi** – (NZ English) crazy
2 **Twisties** – brand of snack food products, similar to crisps

Tasks

- *Read the tasks carefully.*
- *Make sure to write about **all** the aspects presented in each task.*

1. **Summarise** the information given in the excerpt.
2. **Explain** what the incident tells the reader about the four boys' characters. Focus on their behaviour and the way the story is told (narrative technique, use of language).
3. Here you can choose between two different options.

option a)

Comment on Niko's short talk with Miss Martin.

Include the following aspects:
- what students can expect of a teacher and a school in cases of bullying
- Niko's motivation for not telling Miss Martin about the bullying
- what victims of bullying can do

OR

option b)

Write an alternative ending to the story when Miss Martin asks Niko: "Those boys been picking on you?" (l. 40)

Include the following aspects:
- Niko's different reaction to her question
- a student-teacher conversation about the problem of bullying based on trust and honesty
- solutions for creating a safer environment for Niko and other victims of bullying at school

Lösungsvorschläge

1 **HINT**

Bei einer klassischen *summary* kommt es auf einen prägnanten Einleitungssatz (Autor, Titel, Erscheinungsjahr, Thema) sowie eine präzise Zusammenfassung der Ereignisse (v. a. die Auflistung der Misshandlungen in der Toilette und das kurze Gespräch mit der Lehrerin vor dem Schulgebäude) in möglichst eigenen Worten im *simple present* an.

The excerpt taken from the novel *The Pōrangi Boy* by Shilo Kino, published in 2020, deals with the bullying of a young boy named Niko at a school in New Zealand. introductory sentence

Niko is in a cubicle in the school toilets when three boys (Tū, Kaore and Hone) enter and try to open the door. As he cannot escape through the window, Niko quickly opens the door and tries to run away. One of the boys lifts Niko up and pushes him against the toilet. While making fun of Niko, they take one of his books, throw it into the toilet and tell him to get it out. When Niko tries to do so, Kaore and Hone hold onto Niko's arms, while Tū urinates into the toilet. They dunk Niko's head into the toilet bowl, flush the toilet, kick him in the back and leave. attack by the boys in the toilets

Niko grabs his belongings, including the wet book, leaves the building and meets Miss Martin, one of his teachers. encounter with his teacher

Although Miss Martin realises that something has been done to him and asks him about it several times, Niko does not tell her about the incident. Before getting into her car the teacher offers that he can come and see her at the library whenever he needs a quiet place to relax.

2 **HINT**

Für die Charakterisierung der Hauptfigur wie der Täter musst du hier zwischen den Zeilen lesen. Um Rückschlüsse auf den Charakter zu ziehen, solltest du dir die direkte Rede der Figuren sowie die Darstellung ihrer Handlungen genau ansehen. Es empfiehlt sich die komplexe Aufgabenstellung in folgender Struktur zu bearbeiten:

Erzählperspektive *(narrative technique)*

- *first-person narrator → Niko's point of view*
- *no revelation of his inner thoughts or feelings, events presented like a report*

- *conclusions about bullies drawn from Niko's descriptions and their direct speech*

Charakterisierung der Hauptfigur: Niko

- *tough and brave*
- *thinks of an escape plan (ll. 3/4), does not show any weakness on the outside, tries to defend himself ("Let me go!", l. 26)*
- *interested in literature (book:* Matilda, *l. 18; goes to library, ll. 18, 50/51)*
- *may feel ashamed/is probably too proud and does not open up to teacher (cf. ll. 38–52)*

Charakterbeschreibung der Täter: Tū, Kaore und Hone

- *three boys show typical bullying behaviour: act in a group, choose a location with no witnesses*
- *used to bullying → Miss Martin's remark: "Don't you let those boys push you around" (l. 42)*
- *total lack of empathy, no moral compass → brutal and disgusting behaviour/ criminal offences*
- *Tū seems to be in command ("[Tū] nods slightly and Kaore lifts me up" l. 8); exercises most of the violence: "grabs [his] bag and tips it upside down" (l. 12), throws Niko "back on the floor" and his book into the toilet (cf. l. 20), "starts pissing in the toilet" (l. 29)*
- *bullies with inferiority complex → Kaore has "stubby fingers" (l. 2) → weight problems?*

Sprache *(use of language)*

choice of words reflects the brutality of the bullies and their actions

- *Kaore: unpleasant person, "ugly voice [...] stubby fingers" (l. 2)*
- *excessive use of verbs illustrating the quick acts of violence ("shoves", l. 8; "snatches", l. 14; "jerked", l. 25; "pissing", l. 29; "dunked", l. 30; "yanked", l. 31) and the consequences ("gasp", l. 31; "coughing and spluttering", ll. 31/32)*
- *informal word "piss" is used three times (in lines 29, 30, 38), emphasising the brutal act of humiliation*
- *Niko: repetition of "nothing" (ll. 38, 45, 49) → too ashamed/proud/shocked to talk about the incident and accept the teacher's help, maybe also sign of a denial that he is being bullied?*

introduction
thesis

The excerpt from the novel *The Pōrangi Boy* depicts a brutal scene of bullying at school involving three bullies (Tū, Kaore and Hone) and one victim (Niko), whose characters will be the focus of the following analysis. The narrative techniques employed by the author and her use of language will also be taken into consideration.

main part:
narrative techniques

The first-person narrator Niko relates the course of action from his point of view. Interestingly, he presents the incident like a report and does not explicitly reveal his inner thoughts or feelings. Moreover, the reader can only draw conclusions about the bullies from Niko's descriptions of them and their actions and also their direct speech.

character study – protagonist and victim of bullying: Niko

Taking a closer look at Niko's character one can say that he is quite tough and brave. When he senses the threat, he immediately tries to think of an escape route (ll. 3/4) and does not show any weakness on the outside. He tries to run away first and then to defend himself ("Let me go!" l. 26).

Furthermore, the reader learns about Niko's interest in reading, as he has the book *Matilda* (cf. l. 18) with him and goes to the school library (ll. 18, 50/51).

He may feel ashamed or is probably too proud to tell anyone about what has happened. He therefore chooses not to confide in his teacher when she realises that something is wrong (cf. 38–52).

the bullies and their record of crimes

The three boys Tū, Kaore and Hone show typical bullying behaviour as they act in a group and pick a location with no witnesses present.

The way the three bullies interact und enjoy the torture suggests that they may be used to bullying others. Miss Martin's remark "Don't you let those boys push you around," (l. 42) also proves that they have a history of bullying.

The three of them display a total lack of empathy. Their brutal and disgusting behaviour is a criminal offence (cf. ll. 12/13, 20–33).

Tū seems to be in command of the gang, as he tells the others what to do ("[Tū] nods slightly and Kaore […]", l. 8) and he is the one exercising most of the violence when he throws Niko "back on the floor" (l. 20) or "starts pissing in the toilet" (l. 29), to name just two examples.

Bullies themselves are often troubled by an inferiority complex in some department. This might be true for Kaore, whose "stubby fingers" (l. 2) suggest weight problems regarding his physique.

use of language – merciless and straight to the point

The author's choice of words powerfully and accurately mirrors the brutality of the bullies and their humiliating actions.

In the very first sentences, Kaore, one of the bullies, is already depicted as an unpleasant person with an "ugly voice and […] stubby fingers" (l. 2).

This is followed by an accumulation of verbs that illustrate and document the group's quick acts of violence ("shoves", l. 8; "snatches", l. 14; "jerked", l. 25; "pissing", l. 29; "dunked", l. 30;

"yanked", l. 31) and the consequences for their victim ("gasp", l. 31; "coughing and spluttering", ll. 31/32).
The omnipresent informal word "piss" (used three times in lines 29, 30, 38) emphasises the brutal act of humiliation and creates an atmosphere of unease and hostility.

conclusion

The reader is confronted with a group of three bullies with no moral compass. The victim takes the violence without revealing any emotions and neither talks about his physical and mental suffering nor seeks help when the chance is offered. The language reflects the merciless record of crimes committed.

3 **HINT** **option a)**

Diese Aufgabe verlangt von dir, zu Nikos Entscheidung und der Reaktion der Lehrerin Stellung zu beziehen und dabei bestimmte Aspekte zu berücksichtigen. Sammle also zunächst Ideen zu den drei angegebenen Punkten, z. B.:

What students can expect of a teacher and a school in cases of bullying
- *relationship that is supposed to be built on mutual trust and respect*
- *teachers are …*
  - *responsible for the well-being of their students in a safe environment*
  - *trained to counsel students or to offer help*
  - *not doing their job right if they ignore bullying*

Niko's motivation for not telling Miss Martin about the bullying
- *may feel ashamed or too proud to acknowledge that he has been attacked*
- *could be afraid that he would be bullied even more if the bullies found out he had reported the crime*
- *feels humiliated and wants to forget about it quickly*
- *does not want to lose face or be seen as weak in front of Miss Martin, whom he finds attractive and notices things about ("still looks pretty", l. 39; "Her ponytail swings back and forth", l. 53; "She's humming a song", l. 54; "hops into her little red car", l. 55)*

What victims of bullying can do
- *talk to/confide in a close friend/parent/teacher they trust*
- *call a professional helpline for support*
- *document the crimes and go to the police with their parents*
- *defend themselves if possible*
- *should always keep in mind that it is the bullies' fault: they are the ones with the problem*

Unfortunately, Niko finds himself in a situation that numerous students have to endure in schools today: he is exposed to severe bullying at a place which is supposed to be a safe zone for students. He decides not to tell his teacher about the incident even though she is aware of what has just happened and tries to help him.

introduction: topic, brief description of Niko's situation

Of course, students can expect their teachers and schools to take bullying seriously and to have a zero-tolerance policy in that regard. They should feel safe reporting any instances of bullying to their teachers or other staff at school and know that appropriate action will be taken to address the situation. A student-teacher relationship is usually built on mutual trust and respect. I have observed that more and more teachers are even professionally trained to counsel students, which naturally includes victims of bullying. Thus, they will know what to do and can take effective measures to protect them.

main part: what students can expect from teachers/schools

However, Niko may not want to tell Miss Martin about the bullying because he may feel embarrassed, ashamed, or afraid of retaliation. It is important to understand that the feelings are common among victims of bullying, but it is essential for them to reach out for help in order to stop the bullying and prevent it from happening again.

Niko's motivation for not accepting help

Victims of bullying can take several steps to address the situation. I hold the view that one of the most important ones is to speak up and tell someone they trust, such as a teacher, counsellor or parent. They can also document any instances of bullying, including when and where it happened and who was involved. This may help when the crime is reported to the police, where one can also seek help of course.

possible actions for victims of bullying

As far as I know, it is also important for victims of bullying to take care of their own emotional well-being by reaching out for support from friends, family or a professional counsellor. They should always keep in mind that it is the bullies' fault: the bullies are the ones with the problem, not them. Being exposed to bullying can happen to anyone.

conclusion

HINT **option b)**

In Teil b) ist wieder deine Kreativität gefragt. Hier steht ein sich Hineindenken in und ein Umdenken der brenzligen Situation im Vordergrund. Wie könnte das Gespräch auch verlaufen, wenn Niko oder die Lehrerin eine andere Entscheidung treffen? Sammle zunächst Ideen zu den angegebenen drei Punkten und verfasse dann ein alternatives Ende im recht nüchternen berichtenden Stil des Texts mit Niko als *first-person narrator.*

Niko's different reaction to her question

- *Niko can wash his hair, gets a towel*
- *Niko describes what he has endured in the toilets*
- *They go to a quiet place to have a serious and sensitive conversation*

Student-teacher conversation about the problem of bullying

- *Niko admits that this was not the first time*
- *teacher offers support and recommends involving the parents/police/head teacher*
- *teacher explains why some students become bullies*

Solutions for creating a safer environment

- *teacher tries to find out who could help to support/protect Niko at school*
- *teacher makes it clear that Niko has not done anything wrong*
- *teacher and Niko discuss options for how to proceed*

"Those boys been picking on you?"

"Uh … Well …" different reaction

"You don't have to answer that right now. How about we go to the first aid room? You can wash your hair and get a fresh towel. Come on." student-teacher conversation

She smiles and looks pretty, aiming her head towards the building.

She leads the way to the room. She waits outside while I go in, wash my hair and dry it with a towel. It's scratchy but clean. She comes back in.

"Those boys pushed you around again, didn't they? They messed up your hair and the book … Am I right?"

I'm taken by surprise and remain silent. Then I catch myself nodding slightly.

"That's not OK, Niko. And I am sorry you had to go through that. Listen … you're not the only one they've attacked, you know. They have a history of it and the head teacher is working on it too. We won't tolerate it. One victim went to the police with her parents. The bullies are the ones with the problem, not you!

strategies towards a safer environment

Have you got any friends around at school that could keep close to you as support?"
Before I can stop them, tears run down my cheeks. I hate myself for it.
"I can handle it."
"Niko, I can see that, but you don't have to take this. You're a tough guy … a great guy. Clever, strong and sensible. That's what your friends and teachers like about you. And we can put an end to this."
I lower my head. Actually, there are two friends I could ask to stick around more often. And I saw that documentary about bullying on TV. Experts saying that the bullies are often psychos with huge problems at home and stuff … One victim of bullying pressed charges against two bullies and they got in serious trouble. They said bullying can happen to anyone.
Just listening to Miss Martin is a relief.
"Niko? Promise you'll think about this and we'll talk tomorrow in the library? And I'll get you a new copy of *Matilda*, OK?"

PRÜFUNGSAUFGABEN

Zentrale Prüfungen 2021 – Englisch
Anforderungen mit gymnasialer Differenzierung

Erster Prüfungsteil: Hörverstehen

Hörverstehen Teil 1: *The summer plans of Danny Boyle*

Danny Boyle, the teenage hero of William Graham's book "Danny Boyle and the ghosts of Ireland", is looking forward to carrying out his plans for the summer.
Find out more about Danny from the beginning of the audiobook.

© Natalia Chuen. Shutterstock.com

- *First read the tasks.*
- *Then listen to the extract.*
- *While you are listening, tick the correct box.*
- *At the end you will hear the extract again.*
- *Now read the tasks. You have **90 seconds** to do this.*
- *Now listen to the extract and do the tasks.*

1. Danny and his family are about to …
   a) ☐ move to Ireland.
   b) ☐ go on a trip to Ireland.
   c) ☐ get visitors from Ireland.

2. Danny is very interested in …
   a) ☐ science fiction.
   b) ☐ other countries.
   c) ☐ flying vehicles.

3. Danny is the kind of person who is rather …
   a) ☐ shy.
   b) ☐ patient.
   c) ☐ adventurous.

4. Danny dislikes the fact that Melinda is …
   a) ☐ the first-born.
   b) ☐ in his school year.
   c) ☐ an athletic person.
5. Danny reacts to Melinda with …
   a) ☐ anger.
   b) ☐ laughter.
   c) ☐ disinterest.
6. Melinda behaves like a …
   a) ☐ bully.
   b) ☐ know-it-all.
   c) ☐ helpful person.
7. Danny is excited about …
   a) ☐ magical stories.
   b) ☐ strange locations.
   c) ☐ the Irish language.
8. Danny ends the conversation so he can …
   a) ☐ learn new vocabulary.
   b) ☐ get his suitcase ready.
   c) ☐ continue his earlier activity.
9. Danny connects Ireland with …
   a) ☐ bad weather.
   b) ☐ grassy fields.
   c) ☐ traditional clothes.
10. In the end, Danny has a terrible …
   a) ☐ accident.
   b) ☐ argument.
   c) ☐ nightmare.

In 30 seconds you will hear the extract again so you can check your answers.

Hörverstehen Teil 2: *Thomas Caffrey's chocolate world*

Thomas Caffrey's sweet creations are loved by many Irish people. Joe Duffy from RTÉ Radio 1 is talking to his guest Neville about the famous Irish chocolate maker.

- *First read the tasks.*
- *Then listen to the interview.*
- *While you are listening, tick the correct box.*
- *At the end you will hear the interview again.*
- *Now read the tasks. You have **90 seconds** to do this.*
- *Now listen to the extract and do the tasks.*

1. The reason for the interview is …
   a) ☐ an unhappy event.
   b) ☐ a new sweet creation.
   c) ☐ a company's anniversary.

2. Neville is one of Thomas Caffrey's …
   a) ☐ faithful clients.
   b) ☐ close relatives.
   c) ☐ former employees.

3. Making chocolates at Caffrey's is a …
   a) ☐ family affair.
   b) ☐ new business.
   c) ☐ modern industry.

4. Thomas Caffrey went into the chocolate business thanks to a …
   a) ☐ holiday job.
   b) ☐ close friend.
   c) ☐ creative talent.

5. Caffrey's big success came thanks to a …
   a) ☐ new location.
   b) ☐ big wedding.
   c) ☐ business deal.

6. Irish chocolate fans really like …
   a) ☐ Caffrey's crunchy sweets.
   b) ☐ anything made by Caffrey's.
   c) ☐ one of Caffrey's creations in particular.

7. Inspiration for one of Caffrey's creations came from a …
   a) ☐ child's pet.
   b) ☐ children's story.
   c) ☐ child's plaything.

8. Today one of Thomas Caffrey's early creations …
   a) ☐ has a modernised recipe.
   b) ☐ exists in several varieties.
   c) ☐ has completely disappeared.

9. Thomas Caffrey is described as …
   a) ☐ strict.
   b) ☐ big hearted.
   c) ☐ money focused.

10. Caffrey's creations are on offer …
   a) ☐ only in Ireland.
   b) ☐ in some countries.
   c) ☐ anywhere in the world.

In 30 seconds you will hear the interview again so you can check your answers.

Leseverstehen

The family that is enough by Juliet Rix

"If you want to hang out with my brothers you have to be in top form or you'll be destroyed," says Eoin (pronounced 'Owen') Colfer, the second of five boys and author of the hugely successful *Artemis Fowl* books (often described as James Bond with fairies). His relationship with his brothers, he believes, explains the quick, dry humour in his books. His writing style has put his books at the top of many bestseller lists, and so Eoin, who used to work as an Irish primary school teacher, became an international celebrity.

Born in 1965, Eoin grew up in the seaside town of Wexford, Ireland. The household was large, loving and loud. Eoin's father used to take his sons on historical trips. "To keep us from fighting, my dad would tell us all stories about fairies and dragons. He had to keep going because whenever he stopped, me and my brothers were at each other's throats[1]."

Eoin loved comic books, invented his own characters and drew and wrote his own comics when he was young. His interest in writing continued as a love of drama: He used to help his mother (a drama teacher and local actress), learned her lines with her and had parts in Wexford Opera Festival productions.

It is perhaps not surprising that when Eoin started to write books, his brothers became the characters. All five boys are part of the story. In the second *Artemis Fowl* book, four goblins[2] have a fight. Their names are almost identical to those of Eoin's brothers.

Eoin had written three other children's books while teaching at the local primary school in Wexford. He thought that his *Artemis* books would also become successful but only in Ireland. But when his wife Jackie read the manuscript, she knew it was different. She asked Eoin's brothers to take him to a pub and make him promise to get an agent[3]. Convincing their brother was really difficult, but it paid off.

The money was not as big as has been reported, but fame came fast and bigger money followed later. Didn't that change things? "Not as much as you would expect," says Eoin. In Ireland everyone is a writer and people in Wexford aren't interested in wealth and fame: "They've known me for decades, so they don't care." The brothers keep his feet on the ground too, Eoin adds.

Colfer's kids have changed his writing. "My son Finn, for example, is very funny," says Eoin. "He comes up with some great funny remarks and I get a lot of material straight from him." When Finn argues in the back of the car, Eoin doesn't tell stories to stop him. Instead, he tries to remember it for his books.

The realisation that his children would one day read his books also made him think about the violence. "There is a huge fight in the first book. I decided there was no need for that really … Now there are struggles but not much actual violence." The amorality[4] of his hero – the criminal boy *Artemis Fowl* – worried the new father in him too. Over the next four books, *Artemis* develops a feeling for right and wrong. "I don't know how much longer he will stay interesting as a character," admits Eoin. "Once he turns completely good, that's it."

From: Juliet Rix: The family that is enough, Guardian 14 Oct 2006, https://www.theguardian.com/lifeandstyle/2006/oct/14/familyandrelationships.booksforchildrenandteenagers, Copyright Guardian News & Media Ltd 2023

Annotations

1 **to be at each other's throat** – to argue angrily
2 **goblin** – a small scary, fantastical creature
3 **agent** – here: a person who is paid to advertise and sell someone's books
4 **amorality** – a lack of moral principles

You are doing a reading project in your English class. All the students have to present a famous English-speaking author who writes books for young adults. You have come across Irish author Eoin Colfer, creator of the famous Artemis Fowl *books. Who is this man? Find out more about him in the online article.*

*Tick the correct box **and** give evidence from the text by quoting short passages from the text.*

1. Eoin Colfer grew up as an only child.

   This statement is … ☐ true ☐ false

   One piece of evidence from the text:

   ____

2. Colfer's way of writing is influenced by his …

   a) ☐ family.
   b) ☐ former job.
   c) ☐ favourite book.

   One piece of evidence from the text:

   ____

3. Colfer grew up in a household with …
   a) ☐ peace and quiet.
   b) ☐ little entertainment.
   c) ☐ lots of fantastic tales.

   One piece of evidence from the text:

   ____

4. Growing up, Colfer showed little creative talent.
   This statement is … ☐ true ☐ false

   One piece of evidence from the text:

   ____

5. Figures in the *Artemis Fowl* books are based on family members.
   This statement is … ☐ true ☐ false

   One piece of evidence from the text:

   ____

6. When Colfer wrote the *Artemis Fowl* books he …
   a) ☐ kept them secret from his family.
   b) ☐ already had some experience in the job.
   c) ☐ hoped they would become an international hit.

   One piece of evidence from the text:

   ____

7. The *Artemis Fowl* books made Colfer rich overnight.
   This statement is … ☐ true ☐ false

   One piece of evidence from the text:

   ____

8. Because of Colfer's success the people in his town …
   a) ☐ began to ask him for money.
   b) ☐ kept their distance from him.
   c) ☐ behaved like they had before.

   One piece of evidence from the text:

   ____

9. Despite his success as a writer, Colfer has remained a fairly normal person.
This statement is … ☐ true ☐ false

One piece of evidence from the text:

____

10. Daily-life situations with his children are an inspiration for Colfer's books.
This statement is … ☐ true ☐ false

One piece of evidence from the text:

____

11. Because of his children, Colfer's stories have become …
    a) ☐ gentler.
    b) ☐ simpler.
    c) ☐ more exciting.

One piece of evidence from the text:

____

12. Colfer plans to stop writing the series once *Artemis Fowl* is too …
    a) ☐ old.
    b) ☐ nice.
    c) ☐ strict.

One piece of evidence from the text:

____

Wortschatz: *Life without Hearing*

Most people think only old people lose their hearing, but in fact anybody can have a hearing loss. Ellie is a deaf teenager and explains in her blog what it is like to be a deaf teen.

- *Fill in suitable words* ***or*** *tick the correct box.*
- *Give only* ***one*** *solution.*

1. Life without discrimination is a basic human …
   a) ☐ truth. b) ☐ right. c) ☐ justice. d) ☐ legislation.

2. To put that into practice, all existing ____________________ have to be removed to create equality between hearing and non-hearing people.

3. Schools which make all their students feel that they are truly part of the school community are called …

   a) ☐ uniting b) ☐ collective c) ☐ inclusive d) ☐ combining

   schools.

4. Creating a good environment for deaf students not only helps the deaf but other people as well. This way everyone becomes more ____________________ of each other and of what other people need.

5. Sometimes people do not understand me because not many people know sign …

   a) ☐ voice. b) ☐ speech. c) ☐ tongue. d) ☐ language.

6. But fortunately there are many ways of ____________________ with others nowadays. I often write emails or use social media.

7. Social media inspired me to set up this blog. I want to show other deaf people they are not alone with the ____________________ they face in their daily lives.

8. In the last few years I've had the chance to use more advanced hearing technologies that have …

   a) ☐ increased b) ☐ improved c) ☐ developed d) ☐ progressed

   my life.

9. Now I'm old enough to do things on my own. The older I get, the more ____________________ I want to become.

10. Deaf people want to be part of the community, but there are situations in which they feel ____________________ from the others.

11. I fought to make my local cinema deaf …

    a) ☐ friendly. b) ☐ enjoyable. c) ☐ nice. d) ☐ funny.

12. The most important thing that I have learnt is that deaf people can …

    a) ☐ aim b) ☐ win c) ☐ catch d) ☐ achieve

    their goals if they really try.

13. Of course this works out better if they are given ____________________.

Schreiben

The Sound of Silence by Myron Uhlberg

It's 1938. Myron Uhlberg is living with his deaf parents. In the following excerpt from his book "The Sound of Silence", he writes about one challenge he had to face as a child to help his dad get along in the hearing world.

I switched on the radio. We were early. The speaker commented on the careers of the two boxers Joe Louis, also called the "Bomber", and Max Schmeling. I had no idea what half of the stuff meant in spoken English, much less how to translate it into sign[1] for my father.

I knew nothing about boxing. I had never seen a match. Questions, questions, questions. I had so many of them, but I didn't want to let my father down. He needed me to tell him what happened.

By now my father had focused on me like a human microscope. He looked straight at me, examining every detail.

I heard the bell for the first round. The crowd roared[2] like a herd of wild animals, the sound loud enough to wake the dead. My father just sat there, surrounded by silence, eyes focused on my hands, my face, and the radio. He was waiting for my hands to transform the radio broadcast he could not hear.

The fight was on. I tried to sign what was happening, to keep up with what I was hearing. But there was just too much noise coming at me, all crowded together. Besides, my signing vocabulary did not include signs for boxing.

How was I supposed to sign, *The Bomber lands with an uppercut*[3]*. Now he's jabbing*[4] *Schmeling. Jab, jab, jab. Schmeling's eye is closing. Joe Louis is killing him. Another blow in his stomach. Oohh, that one will bring up his lunch.*

My father looked frustrated as he tried to make sense of my incomprehensible signs.

Also frustrated, I jumped to my feet. As I listened to each detail describing the action in the boxing ring, I danced in circles in front of my father. I dropped to the floor. I jumped – imagining what I was hearing.

I heard the announcer scream, *Schmeling can run, but he can't hide. Louis has Schmeling. HE'S DOWN! HE'S DOWN! SCHMELING'S DOWN! He's on the floor.*

I dropped to the floor and lay there with my arms and legs spread out.

Louis is standing over Schmeling.

I jumped up, staring down at the floor.

Schmeling's as still as a stone.

I lay still as a stone.

The referee waves Louis to a neutral corner.

I jumped up and followed his command, taking myself to what I decided was the neutral corner of the room.

ONE.

I signed with emphasis the number one … *TWO* … two … *THREE* … three … *Schmeling's trying to get up* … I fell down. I tried to rise … and continued signing …

FOUR … four … *FIVE* … five … *Schmeling falls back to the floor* … I fell back on the carpet. *SIX* … six … I signed the number from the floor …

SEVEN … seven … *EIGHT* … eight … *NINE* … nine … *TEN* … I made a fist, held my thumb up, and shook my hand furiously … TEN.

It's all over! Schmeling's out! I was signing madly.

The noise from my radio was deafening. I proudly walked around the room, arms raised in victory. The cheering from the radio was music to my ears. My father cheered and stamped his feet on the floor in wild, true joy.

"Great fight!" he signed when he caught his breath. "I understood everything!" I stood there in the middle of the ring, on the carpet exhausted but proud.

From: Myron Uhlberg: The Sound of Silence: Growing Up Hearing with Deaf Parents, *Albert Whitman / Company, Chicago 2019*

Annotations

1 **sign** – *here:* language used by people who cannot hear or talk
2 **to roar** – make a sound like an animal
3 **uppercut** – a hit against someone's chin
4 **to jab** – to hit sb forcefully and quickly

- *Read the tasks carefully.*
- *Make sure to write about **all** the aspects presented in each task.*

1. **Describe** the situation Myron is in one day and how he deals with it.
(8 Punkte)

2. **Analyse** how Myron's feelings change over the course of the story and how they show in his behaviour and thoughts.
In doing so, look at the way the story is told (narrative technique, use of language). *(12 Punkte)*

3. Here you can choose between three different options. **Do only ONE of them!**

option a)

Comment on the title of the book "The Sound of Silence".

Include the following aspects:
- Is it a good title for the book? Why? Why not?
- What can silence between people mean in different situations?
- Would you like to read the book? Why? Why not? *(10 Punkte)*

or

option b)

It's the year 1938: Myron's dad writes a letter to his sister, Anne, about how Myron helped him in this challenging situation.

Write the letter to Anne.

Include the following aspects:

- how he experienced the situation,
- his thoughts and feelings about his son,
- his wishes and hopes for the future.

You can start like this:

Dear Anne, *June 23rd, 1938*
I hope you are well. You aren't really interested in sports and probably didn't listen to the big event yesterday … but I did! You probably wonder how I did that. Well, … *(10 Punkte)*

or

option c)

Later that evening Myron thinks about this special day and his life with his deaf parents. He writes in his diary.

Write his diary entry.

Include the following aspects:

- his thoughts and feelings about this day,
- happy and difficult moments in his daily life,
- his wishes for himself and his family.

You can start like this:

Dear Diary,
What a day – it was hard work but lots of fun at the same time. Dad wanted …
(10 Punkte)

Erster Prüfungsteil: Hörverstehen

Transcript 1 The summer plans of Danny Boyle

Danny Boyle sat in his room with a map of Ireland lying on his bed. He was carefully circling all the destinations where he and his family would be going on their summer vacation. He had circled Dublin, Galway, and other places with magical names like Connemara. Danny carefully ran his fingers across the map like it was a piece of treasure.

Danny loved to read about distant locations, but this was the first time that he would be getting on a plane and travelling to a place that he had only read about or had stared at on a map.

He thought he had been waiting long enough. Danny lived in Rivertown, a small town near the Mississippi River. Not much happened in Rivertown, so Danny was always looking for adventure wherever he could find it.

Ireland was far away. It was a foreign country and that made all the difference to Danny.

Danny was interrupted by his younger sister Melinda. Even though Danny was two years older than Melinda, they were in the same grade. This fact annoyed Danny but amused Melinda who told everyone she met that she had jumped ahead two grades because she was special.

"Are you still staring at that old map? I've been doing something practical," Melinda said. "Go away," Danny said, keeping his eyes on the map.

"Don't you want to know what I've been doing?"

"Does it look like it?"

"Well, I'll tell you anyway. I've been learning some words in the native Irish language," Melinda said proudly.

"But people in Ireland speak English," Danny reminded her.

"Here's one," Melinda continued. "In Irish, Ireland is called 'Eire'. A river is known as 'abhainn'." Melinda said ignoring Danny's response completely.

"Well, you can talk to the fairies there," Danny said.

"There are no such things as fairies. They're just a legend. You know, something that isn't real," Melinda said.

"I know what a legend is," Danny said. "But there are some dark and mysterious places in Ireland that I want to explore. You never know what you might find."

"We'll go wherever Mom and Dad take us," Melinda said. "And that's that."

"Yeah, yeah," Danny said. "Now can I go back to what I was doing?"

"Fine. I'm going to look up more words and begin packing," Melinda said, turned around and went to her room.

Danny had already packed. Even though it was summer, Ireland can be cool and wet, so he had packed a rain jacket and pants and his waterproof hiking shoes. Danny hadn't slept well the night before he and his family went to the airport. He dreamed that he was alone on a windy island surrounded by fireballs that were leading him to the edge of a cliff. He then began falling down towards the ocean below. Just as he was about to hit the rocks at the bottom of the cliffs, he heard his mother telling him to wake up because it was time to get ready.

His adventure was about to begin.

From: William Graham: Danny Boyle and the Ghosts of Ireland, *GreatUnpublished.com 2002*

HINT

In folgenden Textstellen des Transkripts findest du jeweils die Lösungen:

1 "Danny Boyle sat in his room with a map of Ireland lying on his bed. He was carefully circling all the destinations where he and his family would be going on their summer vacation." (Z. 1–3)

2 "Danny loved to read about distant locations" (Z. 6)

3 "Not much happened in Rivertown, so Danny was always looking for adventure wherever he could find it." (Z. 10/11)

4 "Even though Danny was two years older than Melinda, they were in the same grade. This fact annoyed Danny" (Z. 14–16)

5 "'Go away,' Danny said, keeping his eyes on the map. 'Don't you want to know what I've been doing?' 'Does it look like it?'" (Z. 19–21) Man hört an Dannys Stimme, dass er genervt ist von seiner kleinen Schwester, von „anger" (= Wut, Ärger) kann man aber nicht sprechen.

6 Melinda verhält sich ziemlich besserwisserisch. Sie prahlt mit ihren Sprachkenntnissen (vgl. Z. 22–26) und tut so, als wüsste Danny nicht, dass es keine Feen gibt und was eine Legende sei (vgl. Z. 28/29).

7 "But there are some dark and mysterious places in Ireland that I want to explore." (Z. 30/31)

8 "Now can I go back to what I was doing?" (Z. 33)

9 "Even though it was summer, Ireland can be cool and wet" (Z. 36/37)

10 "He dreamed that he was alone on a windy island surrounded by fireballs that were leading him to the edge of a cliff. He then began falling down towards the ocean below." (Z. 38–41)

1. Danny and his family are about to …

   b) ☑ go on a trip to Ireland.

2. Danny is very interested in …

   b) ☑ other countries.

3. Danny is the kind of person who is rather …

   c) ☑ **adventurous.**

4. Danny dislikes the fact that Melinda is …

   b) ☑ **in his school year.**

5. Danny reacts to Melinda with …

   c) ☑ **disinterest.**

6. Melinda behaves like a …

   b) ☑ **know-it-all.**

7. Danny is excited about …

   b) ☑ **strange locations.**

8. Danny ends the conversation so he can …

   c) ☑ **continue his earlier activity.**

9. Danny connects Ireland with …

   a) ☑ **bad weather.**

10. In the end, Danny has a terrible …

    c) ☑ **nightmare.**

Transcript 2 Thomas Caffrey's chocolate world

Joe: Hello and good afternoon and welcome to Culture of Ireland. Sad news for the children of Ireland and chocolate lovers everywhere: Dublin's favourite chocolate creator, the legendary Thomas Caffrey, died yesterday. He will be sadly missed by his family and the children around the country. We have Neville Caffrey, who is Thomas Caffrey's son, on the line. First of all let me say that I am really sorry about the death of your dad, Neville.

Neville: Thank you very much, Joe, and thanks a lot for talking to me.

Joe: Your business is now in its third generation.

Neville: Yeah, that's right. Thomas Caffrey, my dad, had been there making chocolate since 1930, which is incredible.

Joe: How old was he? May I ask?

Neville: 92. He was 92, the last traditional sugar baker. He was born here in Dublin.

Joe: And when did he get involved in chocolate making, Neville?

Neville: Well, it goes back quite a bit. During summers as a little boy he worked in the chocolate factory of his brother William. William was the chocolate maker and manager for a company called Browns. My dad loved making things …

Joe: Mmh.

Neville: His great breakthrough came when he got a contract with a huge chain of shops in the 1950s. And in 1953, he was asked to make the chocolate confections for the crowning ceremony of Elizabeth II in the UK.

Joe: Wow, incredible. Among the many of Caffrey's creations are Ireland's all-time favourite, the Chocolate Snowball. Did your dad invent the coconut kind of creamy ball we love so much?

Neville: Yeah, he did. It's amazing really so many people haven't forgotten. I remember when I was little I was on the floor with my little toy mouse, and my dad picked it up and said, "Can I borrow this?" He went away with it and used it as a model for his Marshmallow Mice. That was the start of the Marshmallow Mice … they were a sensation! They had two eyes in them and a little tail …

Joe: Are they still a big sell?

Neville: The Marshmallow Mice are no longer sold. But the Snowball still is, yeah. It's one that people come in for. It's a nice sweet to have with a cup of tea or coffee.

Joe: So true … What memories do you have of your father?

Neville: I remember that we were a small business in town. I remember as a kid I used to go to the company and my father, who was a very fine man, used to give a few sweets to me, and my brothers and sisters and to other kids. We loved that.

Joe: Oh, I would have liked that, too. So, how is business going?

Neville: Great! We make a wide range of products really. You can also buy our products in Australia, Canada and in the United States. And people often write asking, "Please, could you also send a box of chocolates or marshmallows to other places."

Joe: Brilliant. Tell us, what was your father's favourite product?

Based on: http://www.caffreyschocolates.com/thomas-caffrey.html

HINT

In folgenden Textstellen des Transkripts findest du jeweils die Lösungen:

1 "Sad news for the children of Ireland and chocolate lovers everywhere: Dublin's favourite chocolate creator, the legendary Thomas Caffrey, died yesterday." (Z. 2/3)

2 "We have Neville Caffrey, who is Thomas Caffrey's son, on the line." (Z. 4/5)

3 "Your business is now in its third generation." (Z. 8)

4 "During summers as a little boy he worked in the chocolate factory of his brother William." (Z. 14/15)

5 "His great breakthrough came when he got a contract with a huge chain of shops in the 1950s." (Z. 18/19)

6 "Among the many of Caffrey's creations are Ireland's all-time favourite, the Chocolate Snowball." (Z. 21/22)

7 "I remember when I was little I was on the floor with my little toy mouse, and my dad picked it up and said, 'Can I borrow this?' He went away with it and used it as a model for his Marshmallow Mice." (Z. 24–27)

8 "The Marshmallow Mice are no longer sold." (Z. 30)

9 "my father, who was a very fine man, used to give a few sweets to me, and my brothers and sisters and to other kids." (Z. 35/36)

10 "You can also buy our products in Australia, Canada and in the United States." (Z. 39/40)

1. The reason for the interview is …

   a) ☑ an unhappy event.

2. Neville is one of Thomas Caffrey's …

   b) ☑ close relatives.

3. Making chocolates at Caffrey's is a …

   a) ☑ family affair.

4. Thomas Caffrey went into the chocolate business thanks to a …

   a) ☑ holiday job.

5. Caffrey's big success came thanks to a …

   c) ☑ business deal.

6. Irish chocolate fans really like …

   c) ☑ one of Caffrey's creations in particular.

7. Inspiration for one of Caffrey's creations came from a …

   c) ☑ child's plaything.

8. Today one of Thomas Caffrey's early creations …

   c) ☑ has completely disappeared.

9. Thomas Caffrey is described as …

   b) ☑ big hearted.

10. Caffrey's creations are on offer …

    b) ☑ in some countries.

Zweiter Prüfungsteil: Leseverstehen – Wortschatz – Schreiben

Leseverstehen

HINT

Unter „Evidence" sind als Hilfe für dich in Klammern die jeweiligen Zeilen des Lesetexts angegeben. Diese Angabe wird in der Prüfung nicht von dir verlangt.

1. Eoin Colfer grew up as an only child.
   This statement is … ☑ **false**
   Evidence: Colfer, the second of five boys (l. 3)

2. Colfer's way of writing is influenced by his …
   a) ☑ **family**.
   Evidence: His relationship with his brothers […] explains the quick, dry humour in his books. (ll. 5–7) / when Eoin started to write books, his brothers became the characters. (ll. 19/20) / All five boys are part of the story. (l. 20) / Colfer's kids have changed his writing. (l. 34)

3. Colfer grew up in a household with …
   c) ☑ **lots of fantastic tales**.
   Evidence: my dad would tell us all stories about fairies and dragons (l. 13)

4. Growing up, Colfer showed little creative talent.
   This statement is … ☑ **false**
   Evidence: Eoin […] invented his own characters and drew and wrote his own comics (ll. 15/16) / His interest in writing continued as a love of drama (ll. 16/17) / He […] learned her lines with her and had parts in Wexford Opera Festival productions. (ll. 17/18)

5. Figures in the *Artemis Fowl* books are based on family members.
   This statement is … ☑ **true**
   Evidence: his brothers became the characters. (ll. 19/20) / All five boys are part of the story. (l. 20) / Their names are almost identical to those of Eoin's brothers. (ll. 21/22)

6. When Colfer wrote the *Artemis Fowl* books he …
   b) ☑ **already had some experience in the job**.
   Evidence: Eoin had written three other children's books (l. 23)

7. The *Artemis Fowl* books made Colfer rich overnight.
   This statement is … ☑ **false**

Evidence: The money was not as big as has been reported, but fame came fast and bigger money followed later. (ll. 29/30)

8. Because of Colfer's success the people in his town …

   c) ☑ **behaved like they had before**.

   Evidence: "Not as much as you would expect," (ll. 30/31) / people in Wexford aren't interested in wealth and fame: "They've known me for decades, so they don't care." (ll. 31–33)

9. Despite his success as a writer, Colfer has remained a fairly normal person.

   This statement is … ☑ **true**

   Evidence: Didn't that change things? "Not as much as you would expect," says Eoin. (ll. 30/31) / The brothers keep his feet on the ground too (l. 33)

10. Daily-life situations with his children are an inspiration for Colfer's books.

    This statement is … ☑ **true**

    Evidence: Colfer's kids have changed his writing. (l. 34) / "He comes up with some great funny remarks and I get a lot of material straight from him." (ll. 35/36) / When Finn argues in the back of the car, Eoin […] tries to remember it for his books. (ll. 36/37)

11. Because of his children, Colfer's stories have become …

    a) ☑ **gentler**.

    Evidence: The realisation that his children would one day read his books also made him think about the violence. (ll. 38/39) / "There is a huge fight in the first book. I decided there was no need for that really … Now there are struggles but not much actual violence." (ll. 39–41)

12. Colfer plans to stop writing the series once *Artemis Fowl* is too …

    b) ☑ **nice**.

    Evidence: "Once he turns completely good, that's it." (l. 44)

Wortschatz: *Life without Hearing*

1. Life without discrimination is a basic human …

   b) ☑ **right**.

2. To put that into practice, all existing **disadvantages/obstacles/handicaps/inequalities/barriers/prejudices/stereotypes** have to be removed …

3. Schools which make all their students feel that they are truly part of the school community are called …

   c) ☑ **inclusive** schools.

4. This way everyone becomes more **aware / tolerant / understanding / conscious** of each other and of what other people need.
5. Sometimes people do not understand me because not many people know sign …

   d) ☑ **language**.
6. But fortunately there are many ways of **communicating / interacting / talking** with others nowadays. I often write emails or use social media.
7. I want to show other deaf people they are not alone with the **challenges / problems / conflicts / situation(s) / dilemma** they face in their daily lives.
8. In the last few years I've had the chance to use more advanced hearing technologies that have …

   b) ☑ **improved** my life.
9. The older I get, the more **independent / autonomous / self-sufficient / self-reliant** I want to become.
10. Deaf people want to be part of the community, but there are situations in which they feel **isolated / excluded / separated / apart / distant** from the others.
11. I fought to make my local cinema deaf …

    a) ☑ **friendly**.
12. The most important thing that I have learnt is that deaf people can …

    d) ☑ **achieve** their goals if they really try.
13. Of course this works out better if they are given **support / help / assistance / encouragement / a chance**.

Schreiben: *The Sound of Silence* by Myron Uhlberg

1 **HINT**

Interessant ist bei diesem Romanauszug, dass der Autor des autobiographischen Buchs auch gleichzeitig der Erzähler ist. In der ersten Aufgabe geht es darum, die Informationen im Text zur Situation, in der sich Myron an diesem Tag befindet, und Myrons Umgang mit dieser Situation in möglichst eigenen Worten detailfreudig und gleichzeitig präzise zu beschreiben, um alle acht Inhaltspunkte zu erhalten. Gliedere deinen Antworttext in zwei Teile:

1. Einleitungssatz + genaue Beschreibung der Situation (5 Punkte „Inhalt“)
2. Myrons Umgang mit der herausfordernden Situation (3 Punkte „Inhalt“)

In the literary excerpt taken from the autobiographical novel *The Sound of Silence*, Myron Uhlberg depicts how he tries to explain a boxing match to his deaf father. — introduction

Myron's deaf father wants to follow a boxing match on the radio and asks his hearing son to translate the action in the ring into sign language. Myron is not familiar with the sport and he does not know how to sign certain aspects of the match. — description of the situation

However, he accepts the challenge and tries to help his father by signing as many details as he can. He then decides to imitate and act out the key moments of the fight in the room by using body language so that his father can successfully follow the course of events. — how Myron deals with the situation

2 **HINT**

Im Fokus der Analyse stehen Myrons Gefühle, die sich im Verlauf der Szene wandeln. Arbeite heraus, wie sich diese in seinem Verhalten und seinen Gedanken widerspiegeln. Gehe zudem kurz auf Erzählperspektive und Sprache (z. B. Wortwahl, Syntax) ein, die ebenfalls die Situation und Emotionen für die Leser*innen besser erlebbar machen. Markiere am besten relevante Textpassagen, die du in deinem Antworttext als Textbelege anführen oder in Form eines Zitats einbetten kannst. Vorschlag für die Struktur der Antwort:

1. Einleitung + Myrons anfängliche Überforderung mit der Situation (4 Punkte „Inhalt“)
2. seine erfolgreichen Strategien das Problem zu lösen führen dazu, dass sich die anfängliche Frustration in Stolz wandelt (4 Punkte „Inhalt“)
3. Ich-Erzähler bietet Möglichkeit zur Identifikation und sorgt dafür, dass sich die Leserschaft gut in die Situation hineindenken kann + Wortwahl und Satzbau spiegeln die Hektik und Spannung wider + Fazit (4 Punkte „Inhalt“)

In the following, the protagonist's changing emotional state will be analysed, taking into account the narrative technique and the use of language. — **introduction**

At first, Myron appears to be under pressure and overwhelmed by his father's request for him to translate the boxing match into sign, as he does not know anything about boxing ("I had no idea what half of the stuff meant in spoken English", ll. 2/3). In addition, he is not familiar with the sign vocabulary he would need (cf. ll. 3/4, 16). Myron fears being a disappointment to his father: "I didn't want to let my father down" (l. 6). His hesitant — **main part:** Myron initially overwhelmed → pressure, frustration

behaviour and inner doubts, reflected by his "incomprehensible signs" (ll. 20/21), lead to frustration on both sides (cf. ll. 20–22). Myron realises the importance of the boxing match to his father and spontaneously takes creative measures to portray the action in the match by using animated body language to show what the boxers do in the ring (cf. e.g. ll. 23/24, 28, 30, 32). The successful combination of sign and expressive body language (cf. ll. 36–44) enables Myron's father to follow the action with excitement and "true joy" (l. 47), whereas Myron feels both tired out and pleased with himself (cf. l. 49).

Myron's creative strategies
→ excitement, pride

The choice of a likeable first-person narrator and Myron's perspective very much help the reader to understand the emotions of pressure and failure that trouble Myron towards the beginning of the scene as well as his exhaustion and pride at the end of the match.

narrative technique:
first-person-narrator → possible identification

Furthermore, the narration is marked by a short, precise and sometimes even cryptic sentence structure (cf. ll. 1, 5, 10, 17–19, 26, 29–33, 44), which helps to portray the hectic and fast-moving boxing match that results in the dramatic climax of the countdown (cf. ll. 36–43). In the second part of the text, the repetition of action verbs such as "jab" (l. 18), "jump" (ll. 22, 24, 30, 34) or "fall" (cf. l. 40) and the use of expressive adjectives ("wild, true", l. 47; "great", l. 48, "proud", l. 49) and adverbs (e.g. "furiously", l. 43; "madly", l. 44; "proudly", l. 45) add to the overall dynamics and tension of the scene.

use of language:
hectic, fast-moving scene
→ short/elliptical main clauses
→ repetition of action verbs
→ choice of words

All in all, the author creates drama and a rollercoaster of ambivalent emotions by having the reader experience the course of events through Myron's eyes only.

conclusion

3 **HINT** **Option a)**

Beim Operator „comment“ hast du die Möglichkeit, entweder eine eher zustimmende oder ablehnende Position gegenüber dem Romantitel einzunehmen.

Arguments for the title	***... against the title***
contradictory character (oxymoron: "sound" ↔ "silence") is interesting	*confusing title, you only get a vague idea of the main topic/conflict*

Meanings of silence in general	*... in Myron's life*
• *embarrassment in difficult conversation with another person* • *silence helps you calm down* • *feeling of resignation or weakness*	• *reflects different facets of relationship with his father* • *strong bond as they somehow depend on each other*
Reasons for reading the book	***... against reading the book***
• *find out more about non-hearing people* • *find out about a special father-son relationship*	• *too far removed from my reality* • *difficult to imagine the period Myron lived in – boring?*

I would like to begin by saying that the title grabbed my attention because of its contradictory character. The oxymoron "The Sound of Silence" makes perfect sense when you enter Myron's world, which is different from most people's everyday lives.

introduction: argument in favour of the title

Moments of silence can occur in various situations and evoke all sorts of emotions in interpersonal relationships: when you feel embarrassed or awkward in a difficult conversation with a friend, parent or teacher, for example. In such moments silence can help you to compose yourself and calm down in order to avoid serious conflict. Although I have to admit that sometimes silence can also be interpreted as a sign of a person's resignation or even weakness, in Myron's life, silence reflects different facets of the intimate relationship between him and his father. Sign language, intense facial expressions, gestures or creative body language enrich their communication. I can somehow identify with Myron's wish to make his parents happy and proud. I feel this is a challenge for many of my peers and I am not sure if parents are always aware of the pressure they exert.

main part: different meanings of silence between people

meaning of silence for Myron

That is why I would like to conclude by saying that I would consider reading the novel to find out more about non-hearing people even though the novel is set in 1938, a period which seems far removed from my own reality.

conclusion: reason for reading the book

HINT **Option b)**

Behalte unbedingt im Hinterkopf, dass wir uns **im Jahr 1938** befinden: Die Lebenswelt von Gehörlosen unterscheidet sich deutlich von der heutigen. Achte hier auch auf die korrekten Zeitformen (v. a. *simple present*, wenn du über die Gedanken des Vaters sprichst und *simple past*, sobald über die erlebte Situation berichtet wird; *will-future* für die Wünsche und Hoffnungen). Nachdem der Name von Myrons Vater im Romanauszug nicht vorkommt, darfst du dir für den Abschluss des Briefes einen Namen ausdenken.

- ***How the father experienced the situation:***
  - *short moment of frustration/disappointment when Myron fails to translate the action*
  - *enjoys Myron's creative translation strategies*
  - *boxing match = great experience for him*
- ***His thoughts and feelings about his son:***
  - *high expectations of him*
  - *feeling of pride*
  - *dependent on his son in various situations; too much pressure on Myron?*
  - *impressed by Myron's creativity*
- ***His hopes and wishes for the future***
  - *more moments of joy and lightheartedness with Myron*
  - *less pressure on his son*
  - *greater public interest in needs of non-hearing people and challenges they face*
  - *inventions that make life of non-hearing people easier*

Dear Anne, *June 23rd, 1938*

I hope you are well. You aren't really interested in sports and probably didn't listen to the big event yesterday … but I did! You probably wonder how I did that. Well, I asked Myron to translate the action of the important boxing match on the radio into sign. At first, he had difficulty doing so: I don't suppose he is very interested in boxing and probably doesn't know the sign vocabulary for much of it. Even though he is not to blame for that, I was disappointed and frustrated because at first I could hardly follow the match.

introductory sentences (from the task)

how he experienced the situation

But guess what? Myron suddenly put on a kind of show and started imitating the main events with his body language. It was wonderful and really exciting.

Thinking back to that moment, I'm afraid I'm putting too much pressure on him. I should be grateful and tell him how proud I

thoughts and feelings about his son

am of him more often. I will tell him that I was very impressed by his creativity.

I must admit that sometimes I don't like the feeling of dependence on the people around me. And sometimes I even hate it. I wish I rather had a normal father-son relationship instead like my friends do. I hope that the public interest in deaf people and the challenges we face daily will grow and that we will benefit from technological progress more in the future.

wishes and hopes for the future

How do you feel about that? How can we thank Myron for his efforts and sacrifices?

finishing sentences

Yours,
Louis

closing name

HINT **Option c)**

Berücksichtige wieder, dass wir uns **im Jahr 1938** befinden: Die Lebenswelt von Gehörlosen und die damalige Jugendsprache unterscheiden sich deutlich von der heutigen Situation. Ein eher neutrales Sprachregister ist deshalb für den Tagebucheintrag zu empfehlen. Achte hier auch auf die korrekten Zeitformen (v. a. *simple present* für Myrons Gedanken, *simple past*, sobald du über die erlebte Situation sprichst und *will-future* für die Wünsche und Hoffnungen).

- ***Myron's thoughts and feelings about the day:***
  - *afraid of not living up to father's expectations*
  - *proud of himself, relieved that he managed to cope with the situation*
  - *feels more confident now*
  - *great to see his father happy and satisfied*
- ***Happy moments in his daily life:***
  - *parents pay him respect and show gratitude when he supports them successfully → great feeling, special bond*
- ***Difficult moments in his daily life:***
  - *more obligations and responsibilities than his peers*
  - *sometimes not as free as he would like → would like to spend more time with friends or pursuing his hobbies*
- ***Wishes for himself and his family:***
  - *having less responsibility for his parents*
  - *more carefree and joyful moments for himself and his family in general*
  - *more technical support to solve problems that non-hearing people have →* will make *active participation easier*
  - *more support and understanding in society for disabled people*

Dear Diary,

What a day – it was hard work but lots of fun at the same time. Dad wanted me to translate a boxing match on the radio into sign and the thing is that I have no idea when it comes to boxing and its rules. I felt a lot of pressure as I didn't know the right sign vocabulary and didn't manage to live up to Dad's expectations to start with. The reporter spoke very fast, so it was hard to understand his commentary and to sign simultaneously. I noticed Dad's frustration and became angry myself. Then suddenly the idea popped into my head that I should imitate the boxers' movements. I used the whole room to demonstrate the action. It was hilarious and Dad enjoyed it very much. He said that he had understood everything. I felt so tired but so proud of myself!

beginning (see task)

Myron's thoughts and feelings about the day

Having said that, the constant need to support my parents in their daily lives sometimes feels like a burden. I wish I had less responsibility and more space to do what I want in my free time and spend more time with my friends. They seem to be much more carefree. Sometimes they ask me to come with them and hang out, but unfortunately I have obligations at home.

difficult moments in his daily life

However, it also makes me happy and proud to be able to support my parents – when I translate for them at the doctor's or at other appointments, for example. I guess that has created a special bond between us.

happy moments in his daily life

Besides, some people in our neighborhood are prejudiced or not really aware of the challenges deaf people are exposed to. Maybe there'll be inventions or even laws in the future that'll support and protect disabled people better. That would also make life easier for me too …

wishes for himself and his family

That's all for now.

finishing sentence

Zentrale Prüfungen 2022 – Englisch
Anforderungen mit gymnasialer Differenzierung

Erster Prüfungsteil: Hörverstehen

Hörverstehen Teil 1: *A hockey lesson*

Simone, the main character of Jenny Colgan's book "Class", is new at an all-girls school in Cornwall. You are going to hear an excerpt from the audiobook. In this excerpt, Simone is having her first PE lesson at the new school.

- *First read the tasks.*
- *Then listen to the extract.*
- *While you are listening, tick the correct box.*
- *At the end you will hear the extract again.*
- *Now read the tasks. You have* ***90 seconds*** *to do this.*
- *Now listen to the extract and do the tasks.*

1. At Simone's new school, PE lessons take place …
   a) ☐ daily.
   b) ☐ once a week.
   c) ☐ several times a week.

2. At the beginning of the lesson Simone feels …
   a) ☐ relaxed.
   b) ☐ curious.
   c) ☐ worried.

3. The PE teacher wants the girls to …
   a) ☐ behave fairly.
   b) ☐ take sports seriously.
   c) ☐ focus more on schoolwork.

4. In order to put teams together, the teacher …
   a) ☐ numbers the students.
   b) ☐ lets the students choose.
   c) ☐ hands out coloured bands.

5. Compared to Simone's old school, the new sports area is …
   a) ☐ bigger.
   b) ☐ similar.
   c) ☐ indoors.

6. When it comes to hockey, Simone has …
   a) ☐ a lot of fun.
   b) ☐ no experience.
   c) ☐ a strong motivation.

7. During the game the PE teacher …
   a) ☐ instructs the students.
   b) ☐ observes the students.
   c) ☐ plays with the students.

8. When the players first run towards Simone, she …
   a) ☐ is helpless.
   b) ☐ keeps cool.
   c) ☐ is terrified.

9. Confronted with the other team, Simone reacts …
   a) ☐ passively.
   b) ☐ confidently.
   c) ☐ automatically.

10. It turns out Simone is a …
   a) ☐ bad player.
   b) ☐ careful player.
   c) ☐ talented player.

In 30 seconds you will hear the extract again so you can check your answers.

Hörverstehen Teil 2: *Conkers*[1] *: A traditional seasonal game*

October is conker season in Ireland. Terry of RTÉ radio is talking to Patricia in St. Anne's Park in Dublin about a very well-known game.

- *First read the tasks.*
- *Then listen to the interview.*
- *While you are listening, tick the correct box.*
- *At the end you will hear the interview again.*
- *Now read the tasks. You have **90 seconds** to do this.*
- *Now listen to the interview and do the tasks.*

1. St. Anne's Park is the location of …
   - a) ☐ a coming competition.
   - b) ☐ an ongoing competition.
   - c) ☐ a recently finished competition.

2. You play conkers …
   - a) ☐ in teams.
   - b) ☐ by yourself.
   - c) ☐ against another person.

3. In the game you have to …
   - a) ☐ roll a conker.
   - b) ☐ catch a conker.
   - c) ☐ attack a conker.

4. The game is over when a conker falls …
   - a) ☐ to pieces.
   - b) ☐ to the ground.
   - c) ☐ out of your hand.

5. To prepare for the game, one tip is to choose …
   - a) ☐ old conkers.
   - b) ☐ soft conkers.
   - c) ☐ fresh conkers.

6. The game of conkers started …
   a) ☐ somewhere in Ireland.
   b) ☐ hundreds of years ago.
   c) ☐ as a competition sport.
7. Today some people feel that conkers is a …
   a) ☐ waste of time.
   b) ☐ dangerous activity.
   c) ☐ typical kids' game.
8. One idea of the Irish Conker Championship is to …
   a) ☐ modernise the game.
   b) ☐ connect young and old.
   c) ☐ get people into the fresh air.
9. To take part in the Championship, you …
   a) ☐ should have some skill.
   b) ☐ have to sign up quickly.
   c) ☐ must use your own equipment.

Annotation
1 **conker** – *Kastanie*

In 30 seconds you will hear the interview again so you can check your answers.

Leseverstehen

The power of traditional beliefs

A group of young people are sitting around a table when one of them scratches his nose. "Ah, my nose is itchy[1]," he says. Then he hits his mates lightly and everything is fine again.

If you know something about Irish superstitions[2], you'll understand that traditionally an itchy nose is a sign of an upcoming fight, and that a fight for fun should be carried out to make sure that a real fight will not happen. Many of us hear superstitions like these in the schoolyard or around the family dinner table and carry them on into adult life.

How many others can you remember, now you're thinking about it? Itching on the inner side of your hands – a sign of money to come. Itching on the temples[3] – something will make you cry.

But it's not all about itching. A gap between the front teeth is a sign of a beautyful singing voice. A black spot on the tongue is a sign of telling lies. Many Irish parents who want their children to tell the truth, tell them: "Stick your tongue out so I can see if you're lying". If your ears are "burning", someone is talking about you. If it's the right ear that feels extremely warm, people are talking about you positively, but if it's the left ear, the talk is negative.

In Ireland, the word for superstition is *piseog*, but the word does not only describe simple sayings and unusual beliefs. In old stories everything connected with magic is believed to be a *piseog*.

A classic *piseog* was connected to *May Day*[4] morning. For Irish people *May Day* was the turning of the year from winter into summer, a time for changes. An unkind person could go out on this particular morning and hide old meat in the hay, or old eggs everywhere on your farm. If you didn't find these things, your luck would turn bad. *May Day* was also a time for good changes – washing one's face with dew[5] on this morning would provide people with fresh beauty throughout the year.

These old beliefs, or superstitions, may seem silly to us now, thinking about them in the light of modern science, but they show our psychological needs. And they show how we as humans have thought, felt, and interacted with the world around us and with each other.

Though we can understand the logic behind the origins of some *piseogs*, they survived because of repetition, not because they made sense. When something is done again and again, down through the generations, it becomes not a superstition but a tradition. Traditions are links to the past and a connection through the generations. Based on them, each new family creates their own rituals.

Maybe the old *piseogs* save us from bad luck and bring about good luck, or maybe they don't. We don't know for sure, so it's up to you to decide what to believe in.

Annotations

1 **itchy** – making you want to scratch
2 **superstition** – the belief that something can bring good or bad luck
3 **temples** – the flat parts of your head between your eyes and ears
4 **May Day** – 1st May, a traditional spring festival celebrated in many countries
5 **dew** – drops of water that form outside during the night

Your English class is doing a project on the strange things people in the English-speaking world believe in. You decide to take a closer look at Ireland. The online article above gives you some information.

> *Tick the correct box and give* **one** *piece of evidence by quoting short passages from the text.*

1. In Ireland, an itchy nose stands for future …

   a) ☐ joy.

   b) ☐ trouble.

   c) ☐ friendship.

   One piece of evidence from the text:

   ___

2. In Irish belief, itching can also mean future wealth.

   This statement is … ☐ true ☐ false

   One piece of evidence from the text:

   ___

3. In Ireland, you ask someone to stick their tongue out to check for …

   a) ☐ illness.

   b) ☐ honesty.

   c) ☐ bad thoughts.

   One piece of evidence from the text:

   ___

4. Your ears can tell you what …
   a) ☐ the weather will be like.
   b) ☐ path your future will take.
   c) ☐ other people think of you.

   One piece of evidence from the text:

   ____

5. The Irish expression *piseog* stands for something that is real.
   This statement is … ☐ true ☐ false

   One piece of evidence from the text:

   ____

6. People played tricks on other people on May Day to …
   a) ☐ make fun of them.
   b) ☐ force them to clean up.
   c) ☐ cause problems for them.

   One piece of evidence from the text:

   ____

7. Today we know that old beliefs tell us a lot about people.
   This statement is … ☐ true ☐ false

   One piece of evidence from the text:

   ____

8. Old beliefs still exist today because they …
   a) ☐ make sense to us.
   b) ☐ explain lots of things.
   c) ☐ are practised regularly.

   One piece of evidence from the text:

   ____

9. How people practise these beliefs can vary.
   This statement is … ☐ true ☐ false

   One piece of evidence from the text:

   ____

10. Finally, the author wants the reader to …
   a) ☐ choose what to think.
   b) ☐ pass on the old beliefs.
   c) ☐ forget about superstition.

   One piece of evidence from the text:

   ____

Wortschatz: *Good first impressions*

First impressions can be nearly impossible to change, and they often define the relationship that follows. Here are some useful tips.

- *Fill in suitable words* **or** *tick the correct box.*
- *Give only* **one** *solution.*

Be on time.

1. Someone you are meeting for the first time will not be interested in your …
   a) ☐ excuse b) ☐ pardon c) ☐ alibi d) ☐ proof
   for being late.
2. Arriving early is much better than arriving late, and is the first step towards really ____________________ a great first impression.

Appearance matters.

3. You should ____________________ your outfit to fit the situation.
4. However, always wear something that makes you feel good, happy and ____________________.

Be Yourself.

5. It's important for you to be your authentic self and not …
   a) ☐ simulate b) ☐ disguise c) ☐ pretend d) ☐ pose
   to be someone you're not.

6. Doing this will help you to build …

   a) ☐ faith   b) ☐ trust   c) ☐ belief   d) ☐ credit

   and earn respect from the people you meet.

Have a winning smile.

7. As the saying goes, "Smile and the world smiles with you." But keep it natural: An exaggerated smile could cause ____________________ and get annoying.

Don't forget your body language.

8. Nervousness can lead to unwanted side effects such as nail biting or sweaty palms. By being aware of your nervous …

   a) ☐ customs   b) ☐ routines   c) ☐ habits   d) ☐ patterns

   you can try to keep them under control.

Make small talk.

9. ____________________ some questions that you would like to ask that person might be a good idea.

10. Or take a few minutes to learn something about him or her. Find out if you have anything in …

    a) ☐ cooperation.   b) ☐ combination.

    c) ☐ company.   d) ☐ common.

    This can be a great way to start the conversation and to keep it going.

Be on your best behaviour.

11. It goes without saying that good manners and polite behaviour belong to a good impression. This includes, for example, turning off your mobile phone so that you give the person your ____________________ attention.

Leave them wanting more.

12. If you have a good feeling about someone during a first meeting, don't be ____________________ to say "goodbye for now".

13. If you really …

a) ☐ connect, b) ☐ join, c) ☐ link, d) ☐ blend,

ask to exchange mobile phone numbers and send a follow up message about how nice it was to meet them.

Schreiben

More than cool extract from David Yoon's *"Super Fake Love Song"*

The story is about a boy named Sunny and a girl named Cirrus. Cirrus has just moved to the neighbourhood. Cirrus visits Sunny at his house to get to know him before she starts at Sunny's school the next day.

My big brother's door was always open, because that's how Gray liked things. The door to my room was always shut, because that's how I liked things. My door was boring. My door could have led to anything – a closet, a brick wall, a strange universe.

You only get one chance to make a first impression, Mum liked to say. It was usually shallow[1] advice, but there was a truth to it that I only now realised.

I followed Cirrus, turning left into Gray's room instead of right into mine.

Cirrus made herself at home in my brother's steel swivel chair[2]. She drummed her fingers on her legs, as if she was waiting to be introduced to the room's history.

I started to say something, then stopped.

I started to say something else, then stopped.

I started to –

Cirrus looked at me with a worried look on her face.

"So are you –" she said.

"These are guitars," I said suddenly. I realised I was getting ready to tell a big lie. "They're my guitars."

Cirrus' eyes grew big. "Wait. Are you in a band?"

"Yup," I said. "It's just a little band, but yes: I am."

Cirrus looked at the guitars again, as if they had changed. "Very cool."

I heard none of this, because my lie was still busy bouncing[3] around the inside of my big empty head like a ball. Shocking, how easily the lie had come out of my mouth.

"You're more than cool," continued Cirrus. "You're brave. Most people don't really have hobbies, if they try anything new at all. Most people don't follow their dreams. They forget about them and only remember them again when they are old and lying on their death bed. Then they wonder, 'what was I so afraid of this whole time?' "

"Wow, heavy," I whispered.

Cirrus noticed something behind my guitars [Gray's guitars]: an old Mortals[4] flyer. "Is that you?" she asked.

I cleared my throat, which was already clear. "That's, uh, my old band," I said. "We split up. I'm working on a new thing."

"Cool-cool," said Cirrus, nodding.

Then she flashed me a look.

Not just any look.

The Look.

I recognised the Look from when Gray was still at school. The Look was a particular type of look Gray got often – a combination of burning curiosity and faked disinterest. Everyone wanted to know my brother; everyone pretended they didn't.

The Look was the expression people gave to someone who was doing something well, and with passion. It was an instinctive attraction to creativity – expressed by emojis with little hearts on their eyes. It was falling a little bit in love with people who were making something new with their hands and their imaginations.

I had always wondered what it would feel like to get the Look, and now I realised I had just found out.

The Look was pure deadly sweet terror, and it felt *incredible*.

I instantly wanted another.

From: David Yoon, Super Fake Love Song. G. P. Putnam's Sons Books for Young Readers. 2020

Annotations

1 **shallow** – not deep
2 **swivel chair** – a chair that can turn in different directions
3 **to bounce** – what a ball does when it hits the ground or a wall
4 **Mortals** – the name of a band

- *Read the tasks carefully.*
- *Make sure to write about* ***all*** *the aspects presented in each task.*

1. **Describe** the situation Sunny is in and how he deals with it. *(8 Punkte)*

2. **Analyse** how Sunny behaves towards Cirrus and how she reacts. In doing so, look at the way the story is told (narrative technique). *(12 Punkte)*

3. Here you can choose between three different options. **Do only ONE of them!**

option a)

In the text Sunny remembers his mother telling him: "You only get one chance to make a first impression". What do you think?

Comment on this statement.

Include the following aspects:
- Sunny's situation,
- possible consequences for Sunny,
- further situations in which this is good advice. *(10 Punkte)*

or

option b)

Sunny's brother, Gray, suddenly walks into the room where Sunny and Cirrus are talking.

Write a continuation of the story.

Include the following aspects:
- how Gray reacts when he sees them,
- how Sunny deals with the situation,
- what Cirrus does.

You can start like this:
Suddenly my brother walked into the room. He looked at me. He looked at Cirrus. Then … *(10 Punkte)*

or

option c)

In the evening, Sunny decides to tell Cirrus the truth and writes her an e-mail.

Write Sunny's e-mail.

Include the following aspects:
- the reasons for his behaviour in Gray's room,
- how he experienced the situation,
- promises he makes and hopes he has for the future.

You can start like this:

Dear Cirrus,
You might be a little surprised to get this e-mail from me. … *(10 Punkte)*

Lösungsvorschläge

Erster Prüfungsteil: Hörverstehen

Transcript 1 A hockey lesson

Simone had been shocked to see on her timetable that there were four periods of PE a week. Back at her old school they'd only had one and she had always hated it. Here it was PE nearly every day.

So Simone got changed into the school's sportswear. She was getting nervous. "Oh God, please. Please let them not pick teams." She couldn't live through that.

Miss James, the PE teacher, walked into the changing rooms. "Hello," she said to everyone. "Sit down." The girls sat down.

"Well, our school has a sports tradition to be proud of. I want you to work just as hard here as you do for your university entrance or anything else you do."

She looked around.

"Okay," she said, running down the room and counting the girls off. "One, two, one, two. Team one is playing against team two," she said.

Simone was in team one. She made her way out as slowly as possible.

"You," said Miss James. Simone was looking out at the huge playing fields. There was a running track, several tennis courts, hockey fields. The grass ran on for what seemed like miles down towards the sea. It was beautiful. Absolutely nothing like the grey asphalt field at her old school.

"You," said Miss James again. Simone realised that Miss James was speaking to her.

"I want you in goal," said Miss James. "Do you think you could be useful there?" It wasn't really a question. Simone opened her mouth to say that she had never played hockey before. Then changed her mind and marched off to the far end of the field.

She was lucky that most of the action was taking place at the other end of the field … for now. But she was afraid that the action might soon come her way. She had no idea what she was doing! Miss James was right in the middle of the teams seeing who could play and had talent or who hated it and was too lazy.

Simone realised that the "enemy team" was coming her way.

She started to panic. "Go! Go!" some of the girls were shouting as the action moved closer and closer to Simone's end. She was getting very nervous. Suddenly there was a girl right in front of her. She shot the ball towards Simone. Without thinking, Simone threw herself and her stick at the ball and pushed it back out into the field. A huge cheer went up from the girls in Simone's team. Simone went pink. "Well done," the teacher said. Simone looked around. It must have been an accident. But as the game continued it became clear to her that her goal-keeping skills weren't an accident. She was good at guessing when the ball was coming towards her and from what angle. Her team won easily.

Simone couldn't believe it. It felt like a totally new sensation. Simone was full of pride.

eigene Zusammenstellung nach Jenny Colgan: Class. *Audiobook. Hachette 2011*

HINT

In folgenden Textstellen des Transkripts findest du jeweils die Lösungen:

1 "there were four periods of PE a week" (Z. 1/2)

2 "She was getting nervous." (Z. 4)

3 "I want you to work just as hard here as you do for your university entrance or anything else you do." (Z. 8/9)

4 "'Okay,' she said, running down the room and counting the girls off. 'One, two, one, two. Team one is playing against team two,' she said." (Z. 11/12)

5 "Simone was looking out at the huge playing fields. There was a running track, several tennis courts, hockey fields. […] Absolutely nothing like the grey asphalt field at her old school." (Z. 14–17)

6 "Simone opened her mouth to say that she had never played hockey before." (Z. 21/22)

7 "Miss James was right in the middle of the teams seeing who could play and had talent or who hated it and was too lazy." (Z. 26/27)

8 "She started to panic." (Z. 29)

9 "Without thinking, Simone threw herself and her stick at the ball and pushed it back out into the field." (Z. 31–33)

10 "But as the game continued it became clear to her that her goal-keeping skills weren't an accident. She was good at guessing when the ball was coming towards her and from what angle." (Z. 35–37)

1. At Simone's new school, PE lessons take place …

   c) ☑ several times a week.

2. At the beginning of the lesson Simone feels …

   c) ☑ worried.

3. The PE teacher wants the girls to …

   b) ☑ take sports seriously.

4. In order to put teams together, the teacher …

   a) ☑ numbers the students.

5. Compared to Simone's old school, the new sports area is …

   a) ☑ bigger.

6. When it comes to hockey, Simone has …

   b) ☑ no experience.

7. During the game the PE teacher …

   b) ☑ observes the students.

8. When the players first run towards Simone, she …

   c) ☑ is terrified.

9. Confronted with the other team, Simone reacts …

   c) ☑ automatically.

10. It turns out Simone is a …

    c) ☑ talented player.

Transcript 2 Conkers: A traditional seasonal game

Terry: It's autumn – time to play conkers! Conkers is played with the fruit of chestnut trees which you can find lying on the ground everywhere at this time of year. I'm joined here in St. Anne's Park by a conkers expert, Patricia. She's helping to organise the Irish Conker Championship which takes place here in the park in two weeks. Hello Patricia!

Patricia: Yes! Hi there!

Terry: Now playing conkers … how does that work?

Patricia: Oh, the game is played by two players. Each player has a conker with a hole made in it. The conker is then tied to a strong piece of string. Most players use shoelaces. One of the players stretches his or her arm out, holding the string with the conker hanging from it.
The other player swings their own conker and tries to hit the first player's conker. Basically, they take turns hitting each other's conkers until one finally breaks. So it's important to have the hardest conker.

Terry: And you do something special to the conkers to try to make them harder, right? Because the whole idea of the game is that your conker doesn't break. How do you do that?

Patricia: You can leave it in a dry place for about a year and that will make it harder. And some people bake the conkers to make them harder, or they cook them in salt water or fill them with glue.

Terry: Tell us: where does the game originally come from?

Patricia: Where does it come from? Well, playing conkers goes all the way back to the late 15th century. The first game of conkers we know of was played on the Isle of Wight in southern England. People often played these games in the evening to relax.

Terry: You know, I was amazed that there are still lots of kids who play conkers. Is that what you would expect?

Patricia: I don't think it is like what it once was. You know, I'm a former teacher. The nicest lunch breaks we supervised in autumn were when the children were playing conkers in the yard. But many schools have banned conkers because head teachers are afraid that children might get hurt while playing the game.

Terry: Now Patricia, why is Dublin organising the Irish Conker Championship?

Patricia: We're organising it for two main reasons: The first one is that I feel that children and many adults have been dominated too much by mobile phones and computers. So, we're trying to bring back the outdoors, if you like. And there is no more typical Irish outdoor sport than conkers! Now the other reason is that we want to attract tourists to the area.

Terry: So if I just come along here the week after next? Do I have to bring anything?

Patricia: Absolutely nothing.

Terry: Not even a conker, no?

Patricia: No, all you need is a good steady hand.

Terry: Ah, okay, well … thank you very much indeed and good luck to all the players next week.

eigene Zusammenstellung nach https://www.rte.ie/lifestyle/nature/2018/1016/1003578-have-you-heard-of-the-all-ireland-conker-cone-championship/

HINT

In folgenden Textstellen des Transkripts findest du jeweils die Lösungen:

1 "She's helping to organise the Irish Conker Championship which takes place here in the park in two weeks." (Z. 3–5)
2 "Oh, the game is played by two players." (Z. 8)
3 "The other player swings their own conker and tries to hit the first player's conker." (Z. 12/13)
4 "they take turns hitting each other's conkers until one finally breaks." (Z. 13)
5 "You can leave it in a dry place for about a year and that will make it harder." (Z. 18/19)
6 "Well, playing conkers goes all the way back to the late 15th century." (Z. 22/23)

7 "But many schools have banned conkers because head teachers are afraid that children might get hurt while playing the game." (Z. 30/31)

8 "So, we're trying to bring back the outdoors, if you like. (Z. 35)

9 "No, all you need is a good steady hand." (Z. 42)

1. St. Anne's Park is the location of …

   a) ☑ a coming competition.

2. You play conkers …

   c) ☑ against another person.

3. In the game you have to …

   c) ☑ attack a conker.

4. The game is over when a conker falls …

   a) ☑ to pieces.

5. To prepare for the game, one tip is to choose …

   a) ☑ old conkers.

6. The game of conkers started …

   b) ☑ hundreds of years ago.

7. Today some people feel that conkers is a …

   b) ☑ dangerous activity.

8. One idea of the Irish Conker Championship is to …

   c) ☑ get people into the fresh air.

9. To take part in the Championship, you …

   a) ☑ should have some skill.

Zweiter Prüfungsteil: Leseverstehen – Wortschatz – Schreiben

Leseverstehen

1. In Ireland, an itchy nose stands for future …

   b) ☑ trouble. Evidence: an itchy nose is a sign of an upcoming fight (l. 5)

2. In Irish belief, itching can also mean future wealth.

   This statement is … ☑ **true**

Evidence: Itching on the inner side of your hands – a sign of money to come. (ll. 9/10)

3. In Ireland, you ask someone to stick their tongue out to check for …
   b) ☑ honesty.
   Evidence: A black spot on the tongue is a sign of telling lies. (l. 13) / "Stick your tongue out so I can see if you're lying". (ll. 14/15)

4. Your ears can tell you what …
   c) ☑ other people think of you.
   Evidence: If it's the right ear that feels extremely warm, people are talking about you positively, but if it's the left ear, the talk is negative. (ll. 16/17)

5. The Irish expression *piseog* stands for something that is real.
   This statement is … ☑ **false**
   Evidence: the word for superstition is *piseog* (l. 18) / everything connected with magic is believed to be a *piseog* (ll. 19/20)

6. People played tricks on other people on May Day to …
   c) ☑ cause problems for them.
   Evidence: If you didn't find these things, your luck would turn bad. (ll. 24/25)

7. Today we know that old beliefs tell us a lot about people.
   This statement is … ☑ **true**
   Evidence: they show our psychological needs (l. 29) / they show how we as humans have thought, felt, and interacted (l. 30)

8. Old beliefs still exist today because they …
   c) ☑ are practised regularly.
   Evidence: they survived because of repetition (ll. 32/33) / When something is done again and again, […] it becomes […] a tradition. (ll. 33–35)

9. How people practise these beliefs can vary.
   This statement is … ☑ **true**
   Evidence: each new family creates their own rituals (l. 36)

10. Finally, the author wants the reader to …
    a) ☑ choose what to think.
    Evidence: it's up to you to decide what to believe in (ll. 38/39)

Wortschatz: *Good first impressions*

1. Someone you are meeting for the first time will not be interested in your …

   a) ☑ **excuse** for being late.

2. Arriving early is much better than arriving late, and is the first step towards really **creating/making/forming/giving/providing/conveying** a great …

3. You should **adjust/choose/pick/change/select/modify** your outfit to fit the situation.

4. However, always wear something that makes you feel good, happy and **comfortable/confident/relaxed**.

5. It's important for you to be your authentic self and not …

   c) ☑ **pretend** to be someone you're not.

6. Doing this will help you to build …

   b) ☑ **trust** and earn respect from the people you meet.

7. As the saying goes, "Smile and the world smiles with you." But keep it natural: An exaggerated smile could cause **confusion/a misunderstanding/ irritation/insecurity/a bad feeling/anger/trouble** and get annoying.

8. Nervousness can lead to unwanted side effects such as nail biting or sweaty palms. By being aware of your nervous …

   c) ☑ **habits** you can try to keep them under control.

9. **Preparing/Formulating/Writing down/Thinking up/Coming up with/ Noting down** some questions that you would like to ask …

10. Or take a few minutes to learn something about him or her. Find out if you have anything in …

    d) ☑ **common**. This can be a great way to …

11. It goes without saying that good manners and polite behaviour belong to a good impression. This includes, for example, turning off your mobile phone so that you give the person your **full/complete/whole/entire/undivided/ focused/concentrated** attention.

12. If you have a good feeling about someone during a first meeting, don't be **afraid/too shy/scared/frightened** to say "goodbye for now".

13. If you really …

    a) ☑ **connect**, ask to exchange mobile phone numbers and …

Schreiben: *More than cool*

1 **HINT**

In dieser Aufgabe geht es darum, die Informationen im Text zu Sunnys Situation und sein Verhalten in möglichst eigenen Worten sachlich und präzise zu beschreiben, um alle acht Inhaltspunkte zu erhalten. Beim Lesen des Texts sollten die entsprechenden Passagen am besten in einer bestimmten Farbe markiert werden. Anschließend kann der Antworttext in zwei Teile gegliedert werden:

1. Einleitungssatz + die genaue Situation: erstes Treffen zwischen Sunny und Cirrus, Cirrus verwechselt die Zimmer (3 Punkte „Inhalt")
2. Wie Sunny mit der Situation umgeht: gibt sich für seinen Bruder aus, klärt das Missverständnis nicht auf, genießt Cirrus' Bewunderung (5 Punkte „Inhalt")

The literary excerpt from the novel *Super Fake Love Song* written by David Yoon deals with the first meeting between the teenage boy Sunny and a girl named Cirrus at Sunny's home. *(introduction)*

Cirrus walks straight into Sunny's big brother's room without knowing whose room it is. Sunny has Cirrus believe that they are in his room and does not reveal the truth about it. He pretends that the guitars in the room are his and that he plays the guitar in a band. Cirrus is fascinated by this and looks up to Sunny, who greatly enjoys her admiration. *(situation, Sunny's way of dealing with it)*

2 **HINT**

Im Fokus der Analyse stehen Sunnys Verhalten und Cirrus' Reaktion darauf. Zudem sollte kurz auf die Erzählperspektive und die Konsequenzen für die Leserschaft eingegangen werden. Es macht also Sinn, in einer anderen Farbe relevante Textpassagen zu markieren, die man im Antworttext auch als Textbelege anführen kann oder in Form eines Zitats einbettet. Die Analyse kannst du in drei Teile gliedern:

1. Einleitung + Erläuterung: Sunnys gemischte Gefühle und seine Entscheidung zur Unwahrheit (4 Punkte „Inhalt")
2. Interpretation: Cirrus' selbstbewusster Auftritt und ihre Reaktion voller Bewunderung für Sunny (4 Punkte „Inhalt")
3. Effekt der Perspektive des Ich-Erzählers (Sunny) sowie z. B. die dazu im Kontrast stehenden hohen Redeanteile von Cirrus im Gespräch der beiden + Fazit (4 Punkte „Inhalt")

In the following analysis the narrator's behaviour towards Cirrus, her reaction to it and the effect of narrative techniques will be examined closely.

introduction

Sunny intends to make a good first impression on Cirrus (cf. ll. 5/6), is nervous and insecure at the beginning of their encounter and does not really know how to get the conversation going. He makes several clumsy attempts at saying something (cf. ll. 10–12).

main part:
Sunny's behaviour: nervous, insecure

The misunderstanding regarding the room is his chance to create an image of himself that is creative and cool. That is why he decides to maintain the lie and even pretends to play the guitar in a band (cf. ll. 15/16, 18). He clearly feels uncomfortable and a bit out of his mind as the lie is "bouncing around the inside of [his] big empty head like a ball" (ll. 20/21).

Sunny's lie: pretends to be someone he is not

Cirrus, by contrast, is at ease, self-confident (cf. ll. 8/9) and straightforward, saying "You're brave. Most people don't really have hobbies, if they try anything new at all", (ll. 23/24). She does not hide her admiration for Sunny's fabricated hobby and calls him "cool" several times (ll. 19, 23, 33). She even flashes him a special look of "burning curiosity and faked disinterest" (ll. 38/39).

Cirrus' reaction: self-confident, full of admiration

The first-person narration only gives insight into Sunny's thoughts and feelings. Sunny is quite shy and reserved and has difficulty making small talk to break the ice (cf. ll. 10–12), for example. The fact that he is the narrator helps to emphasise the contrast to Cirrus' self-confident personality: unlike Cirrus, Sunny seems insecure and troubled by his spontaneous lie and hardly speaks. He whispers (cf. l. 28) and clears his throat (l. 31) whereas Cirrus asks him questions and speaks her mind (e. g. ll. 17, 23–27, 30).

effect of first-person narration: contrast between characters

Moreover, the perspective means that the reader can understand the reason why Sunny does not stick to the truth: he is too intrigued by "*the Look*" (e. g. l. 36) given by Cirrus, which feels "*incredible*" (l. 47).

insight into Sunny's mind: motivation for his behaviour

In a nutshell, Sunny, a rather timid person, cannot resist the temptation to create a fake image of himself to impress a self-assured girl. The narrative technique of the first-person narrator with a limited point of view enables the reader to understand his motives for doing so.

conclusion

3 **HINT** **Option a)**

Du hast hier die Möglichkeit, entweder eine eher zustimmende oder ablehnende Position zur Aussage der Mutter einzunehmen. Entscheidend sind überzeugende Begründungen dafür, die du am Beispiel von Sunnys Situation und kurz anhand deines Erfahrungsschatzes erläuterst und in einer logischen Struktur darstellst.

- ***Sunny's situation***
  - *important for him to make a good first impression on a girl*
  - *needs to decide what kind of impression he wants to make on Cirrus*
  - *seems to be under pressure to impress Cirrus, which makes him lie to her*
- ***Possible consequences for Sunny***
  - *on the one hand: maintaining the lie may result in a first date with Cirrus; gaining self-confidence, Sunny may feel ready to really learn to play the guitar*
  - *on the other hand: Cirrus could turn away/break off contact when she finds out about the lie; Cirrus could tell other students about Sunny's lame attempt at connecting with her; Sunny might get in trouble with his brother when he finds out about it*
- ***Further situations***
  - *job interviews*
  - *first date, first meeting/encounter with your girl-/boyfriend's parents*
  - *new environments in your professional and private life*

introduction

"You only get one chance to make a first impression." On taking a closer look at Sunny's dilemma, my first impulse is to agree with that statement.

main part: Sunny's situation

Sunny is under so much pressure to make a good first impression on Cirrus that he feels he has to tell lies and pretend to be someone he is not. He also decides to stick to that story. Maybe this strategy will help him to arrange a first date with Cirrus or maybe he will now be motivated to take guitar lessons and become more self-confident. You never know.

possible consequences

However, as soon as Cirrus finds out about the hoax, Sunny will probably face unpleasant consequences: Cirrus might turn her back on him or, even worse, she could tell their classmates about Sunny's desperate attempt to impress her, and he would be a laughing stock at school. His brother Gray will definitely not be amused either. Sunny risks never being offered a second chance.

First impressions do play an important role in interpersonal relationships because that is when you decide if you can trust someone or not – whether that is at a job interview or on a first date or when you move to a new neighbourhood.

further situations

In conclusion, I would like to say that Sunny's mother is quite right about first impressions. What is more, Sunny should not have to be afraid of being himself. Honesty, a good sense of humour and authenticity are the keys to long-lasting, healthy relationships and if a person is not interested in who you really are, they might miss the chance of gaining a good friend or colleague.

conclusion

HINT **Option b)**

Du hast hier die Möglichkeit einen dramatischen und konfliktgeladenen Höhepunkt zu kreieren (Gray lässt Sunny auffliegen – Wie reagiert Cirrus darauf? Wie verhält sich Sunny?) oder aber eine überraschende und amüsante Zuspitzung zu inszenieren (Gray lässt sich auf Sunnys Spiel ein – Was macht Cirrus?). Wichtig ist dabei, dass du den Stil des Romans beibehältst: Führe den Handlungsfaden aus der Perspektive von Sunny weiter und schreibe dabei im *simple past*. Verwende wörtliche Rede für die weiteren anwesenden Charaktere.

Suddenly my brother walked into the room. He looked at me. He looked at Cirrus. Then he smirked and asked, "What are you two lovebirds doing here?"

Gray's first reaction when he sees Sunny and Cirrus

I almost had a heart attack, quickly pulled myself together, had to clear my throat (for real this time) and answered in a rather high-pitched voice, "Hey brother, meet Cirrus from next door. I'm showing her my guitar and we're talking about my time with the Mortals".

how Sunny deals with the stressful situation

What the hell was I doing? The lies just kept popping out of my mouth.

We both looked at Gray and Cirrus didn't notice the desperate look in my eyes directed at my big brother.

"I'm Cirrus, nice to meet you," she said.

Cirrus' response

"Can I help you with anything?" I asked shakily.

Awkward moment of silence. I was holding my breath.

"Well, Sunny, uh …, I'm Gray, by the way, I was wondering if I could borrow that cool book about rock music you mentioned recently …?" Gray had a subtle grin on his face.

how the conflict unfolds unexpectedly

"Yeah, of course. I'm just not sure where I put it exactly," I heard myself say.

"Is it the one on *your* desk next to the laptop?" Now, Gray was definitely smiling.
"Oh yeah" I said, using my best matter-of-fact tone.
"You must be so proud of your brother. Being in a band and all that. Guess a lot of artists come to your house …" Cirrus stood up from the swivel chair and obviously intended to fetch the book from the desk, when I remembered the framed photo of Gray and his band that was standing right next to the laptop.

HINT **Option c)**

Hier musst du näher am Text bleiben und kannst weniger kreativ formulieren. Halte dir daher erneut Sunnys Beweggründe und sein grundsätzlich schüchternes Wesen vor Augen, um in der E-Mail den richtigen Ton zu treffen.

- ***Reasons for his behaviour***
  - *felt the urge to make a good impression*
  - *missed "the point of no return", could not find the right moment to tell the truth*
  - *enjoyed appearing more interesting and creative*
- ***How he experienced the situation***
  - *surprised that Cirrus went into his brother's room*
  - *became nervous and a bit insecure*
  - *used the opportunity to create a positive image of himself*
  - *somehow enjoyed being in his brother's shoes and the admiration he got in return*
- ***Promises and hopes for the future***
  - *promise to stick to the truth*
  - *hope to be offered a second chance to get to know Cirrus better and to show her who he really is → apology*
  - *Sunny hopes to save the embarrassing situation/to befriend Cirrus*

Dear Cirrus, — see task

You might be a little surprised to get this e-mail from me. I won't beat around the bush. I was happy to meet someone my age in the neighbourhood and intended to make a good impression on you. I must admit that some of the things you learned about me are not true at all and I would like to apologise for that. — admitting the lie, apology

To be honest, you walked straight into my big brother's room instead of mine and <u>he</u> is the musician in the family not me. I kind of got nervous and carried away by the dynamics of the conversation and the idea of being someone else – someone who is — reasons for his behaviour

interesting, cool and creative. I liked your curiosity about me being an artist and I hope all that doesn't sound like a lame excuse …

On reflection, I realise I should have stuck to the truth right away when the stupid guitars came up. I'm so sorry. | apology

From now on, I can only promise to tell you the truth and I would totally understand if you decided to stop all contact. | promises and hopes for the future

I'd be more than happy to show you around the city and tell you about my hobbies and who I really am. I also hope we can keep this between the two of us.

By the way, my brother's band is playing next weekend. They're awesome on stage. We could go and see them … start over. How do you feel about it?

See you, | closing

Sunny | name

Zentrale Prüfungen 2023 – Englisch
Anforderungen mit gymnasialer Differenzierung

Um dir die Prüfung 2023 schnellstmöglich zur Verfügung stellen zu können, bringen wir sie in digitaler Form heraus.
Sobald die Original-Prüfungsaufgaben 2023 freigegeben sind, kannst du sie als PDF auf der Plattform **MyStark** herunterladen (Zugangscode vgl. Umschlaginnenseite, vorne im Buch).

Aktuelle Prüfung

www.stark-verlag.de/mystark